MIGHTY MORPHIN
POWER
RANGERS ™
3

The Power Rangers have powered-up with some new additions. Tommy returns as the White Ranger™ and with him, he brings the new White Tigerzord™. With this new member on the team, the Power Rangers are sure to shock their new enemy, Lord Zedd™ and his followers.

A NEW HERO WHITE RANGER™

The new hero, White Ranger, has joined the Power Rangers team to help them fight their new enemy, Lord Zedd™. His new armor around his chest, arms and legs protect him from enemy attacks. With his new and improved moves, Tommy is better than ever.

Though Tommy lost his powers as the Green Ranger™ to Zedd, Zordon™ replaces his powers and Tommy returns as the White Ranger. His martial arts moves are sure to give the enemies a great punch!

This is where the White Ranger controls the White Tigerzord.

THE WHITE TIGERZORD

Commanded by the White Ranger™, the White Tigerzord can transform from its tiger form to a robot. Depending on which is better for the job, the White Tigerzord is able to morph from one to the other.

Red Dragon Thunderzord™

The Red Ranger™ pilots the new fire-breathing Red Dragon Thunderzord. Its powerful claws can shred anything it can grab a hold of. It can also shoot a stream of fire from its mouth, torching everything in its path.

Unicorn Thunderzord™

Controlled by the Blue Ranger™, the Unicorn Thunderzord is able to fly. With his new Thunderzord, Billy will fight for victory against Lord Zedd™ and his horrid followers.

THUNDERZORDS™!!

In addition to the new White Ranger, the original members of the Power Rangers™ squad have also acquired some new weapons of their own. The Dinozords™ have powered-up to become the Thunderzords™.

Flown by the Pink Ranger™, the Fire Bird Thunderzord replaces the Pterodactyl Dinozord. Kimberly's new Thunderzord is able to fly at very high speeds.

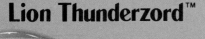

Fire Bird Thunderzord™

Lion Thunderzord™

Griffin Thunderzord™

Zack will drive the Lion Thunderzord™. With its heavy armor, the Black Ranger™ and his Thunderzord should be able to withstand just about any attack.

The Yellow Ranger, Trini, will pilot the Griffin Thunderzord™. Its sleek form will enable Trini and her new Thunderzord to keep the agility that the Sabertooth Tiger Dinozord had.

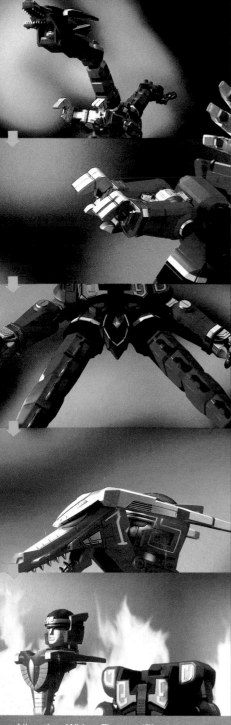

Like the White Tigerzord™, the Red Dragon Thunderzord is able to transform into robot form. These two robots are unique in that they can alter their structures.

Jason's new Red Dragon Thunderzord™ is one of the most powerful Zords™ ever to be created. With Rita banished by Lord Zedd™, you can count on the monsters brought on by Lord Zedd to be much stronger. Jason and his crew will need all the help he can get from the new Thunderzords™.

The Red Dragon Thunderzord flying through the air.

The fly-kicking Red Dragon Thunderzord in its humanoid form.

THE RED DRAGON THUNDERZORD™ ATTACKS!

Like the Dinozords™, the five Thunderzords™ can combine to make the Mega Thunderzord. The different skills that each Thunderzord brings makes the Mega Thunderzord a great fighter.

THUNDER MEGAZORD™

The five Thunderzords combine to make the Mega Thunderzord!

When Tommy returns as the White Ranger™ and brings with him the White Tigerzord™, the Thunderzords are able to combine with it to make the Mega Tigerzord. Extra Zords™ means extra power! The all new Mega Tigerzord is invincible!! Watch out Lord Zedd™!

The All New
MEGA TIGERZORD™

With Tommy's new White Tigerzord™ the Thunder Megazord morphs into the Mega Tigerzord!

LORD ZEDD™!!
This new enemy has awesome powers but the Power Rangers™ will never back down.

"Ground to Pilot: Maintain Your Course!"

Like the crew of a large military aircraft, a Telsen-Sao astral travel team includes both a pilot and a navigator. And as the journey begins, a guide comparable to an air-traffic controller offers flight instructions that only the initiated know how to apply: "Rudder completely up. Correct six degrees to the right. Good, proceed."

According to Jeshahr, the pilot alone embarks on the actual out-of-body experience. The navigator remains behind, serving as a communications link between pilot and guide and, in theory, supplementing the pilot's efforts with extra psychic power. Even with that assistance, pilots are reportedly so quickly exhausted that school policy limits all flights to no more than twenty-eight minutes.

On cots in Telsen-Sao's "astro-dynamic laboratory," two cadets wearing copper breastplates said to draw on their electromagnetic fields start an astral journey. As the pilot (below, left) separates mind and body, the navigator (right) is said to provide a boost of "lymph energy" through electric circuits linking the cadets.

Unique Creations from Troubled Talents

A small pavilion on a hillside, the Haus der Künstler is surrounded by meadows, fields, and woods. In this idyllic setting, mental patients paint, draw, and write in response to urges that may not be unlike those that drive artists everywhere.

The Haus der Künstler was founded in 1981 by Dr. Leo Navratil, the director of the psychiatric hospital in Gugging, who was impressed by the talent his patients displayed in diagnostic drawing tests. Navratil established an environment where their creativity would be given free rein; there are no studios, no fixed hours. The resulting work shows virtually no influence by other artists, reflecting only the personalities and dispositions of the individual residents.

Figures, emblems, and slogans crowd the walls and ceiling of August Walla's room in the Haus der Künstler (below). Dr. Navratil has said of Walla that he "lives in a permanent fear of death, God, spirits and man. Through his artwork, he has been able to fend off these dangers to a certain degree."

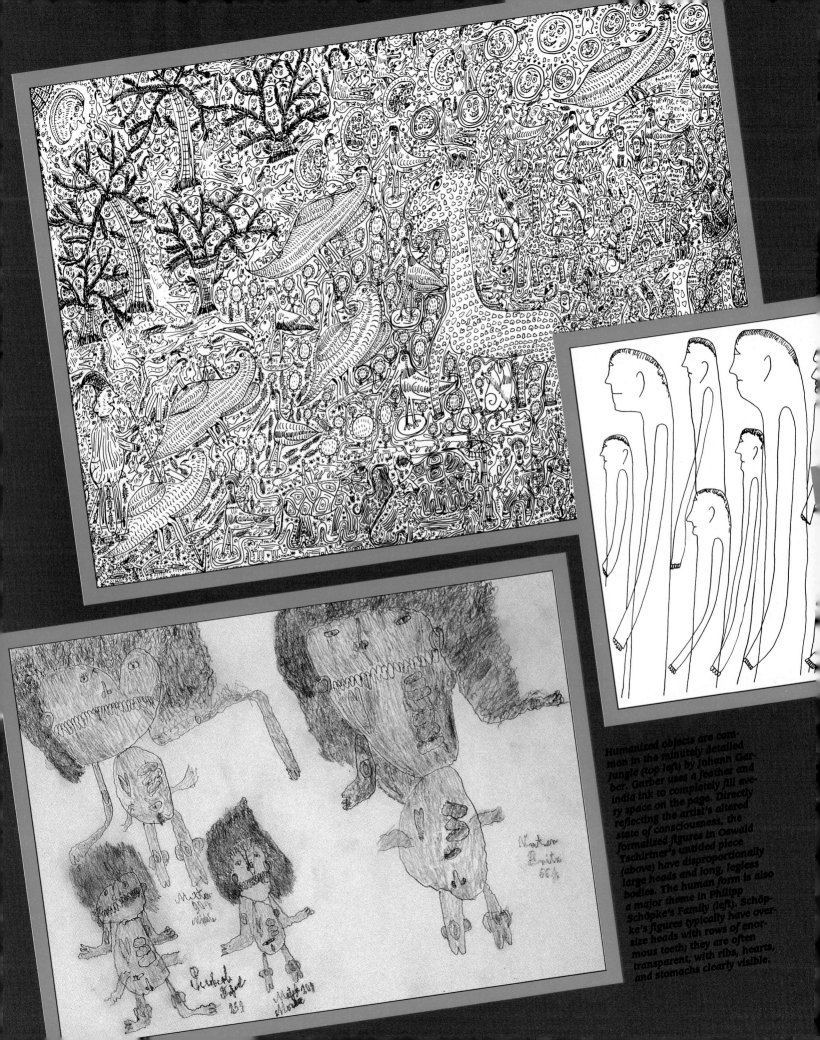

Humanized objects are common in the minutely detailed jungle (top left) by Johann Garber. Garber uses a feather and india ink to completely fill every space on the page. Directly reflecting the artist's altered state of consciousness, the formalized figures in Oswald Tschirtner's untitled piece (above) have disproportionally large heads and long, legless bodies. The human form is also a major theme in Philipp Schöpke's *Family* (left). Schöpke's figures typically have oversize heads with rows of enormous teeth; they are often transparent, with ribs, hearts, and stomachs clearly visible.

Franz Kernbeis 1988.

KOLLeR SeLBStPORTRe. 28 MÄRZ. 1990.
FRITZ.

As simple and flat as a prehistoric cave drawing, Stag by Franz Kernbeis (left) has a clearly human face. The abstract Self Portrait (below left on this page) by Fritz Koller incorporates recognizable fragments of human forms as well as geometric shapes—considered by some to demonstrate the disintegration of his personality. Tables (below), a work by Heinrich Reisenbauer, is an extreme example of formalization, a clear effort to impose order on a confused mind.

Common Threads in Uncommon Visions

The thoroughly individual styles of outsider artists share features that reflect the most dramatic (but not the most serious) symptoms of schizophrenia. Dr. Navratil identified three main characteristics—humanization, formalization, and symbolization—pervading his patients' art. In humanization, emotional attributes are displaced onto inanimate objects, which may have humanlike faces or be deformed in some telling way. Formalization, expressed in geometric forms or repetition of stereotyped patterns, reflects a yearning to restore structure to the disordered mind. Symbolization is the process by which humanized objects begin to assume a constant meaning in the artist's mind, at first mysterious but finally completely rational.

Two drawings on the theme of rockets (near right) reveal the months-long mood swings that characterize Johann Hauser's illness. In a manic state, the artist displays an expansive style, full of detail and bright colors and signed with great confidence; by contrast, the depressed Hauser produced a flat, static, monochromatic rocket. Woman with Feather Hat and Colorful Skirt (far right) illustrates the artist's approach to a favorite subject. Hauser's women are at once feminine and frightening, portrayed in bold, expressive colors with breasts that look like rockets.

A Manic-Depressive's Wild Swings of Style

The colorful drawings of Johann Hauser are among the most important works by outsider artists. A manic-depressive, Hauser was first committed to a hospital at age seventeen. He was thirty-three in 1959 when Dr. Navratil invited him to begin drawing, an activity he has pursued diligently ever since. His symptoms improved after he turned to art, but Hauser remains dependent on the hospital.

Hauser's art, which changes with the phases of his illness, manifests the deepest levels of his internal reality. He seems aware that his images are an effective way for him to reach out to others. In any event, Hauser's style is influential at Gugging, where his picture of a blue star on a white ground has become the symbol of the Haus der Künstler.

JOHANN HAUSER

CHAPTER 3

A Crowd inside the Head

When he was arrested near Columbus, Ohio, in 1977 for a series of rapes, twenty-two-year-old Billy Milligan seemed unsure of whether he was guilty. A high-school dropout who had recently lost his job as a maintenance worker, Milligan looked dazed and helpless. As he awaited trial, however, his demeanor changed often and dramatically. On two occasions he attempted suicide—once by banging his head against a wall, once by smashing a toilet bowl and cutting his wrists with the porcelain shards. Yet the same man watched with childish delight as cockroaches cavorted in his jail cell.

In a revealing series of interviews, psychologist Dorothy Turner uncovered the startling reason for Milligan's many moods. Billy himself, she found, was just one of several distinct personalities who alternately took control of the young man's body. In time, one alter ego confessed to committing the rapes, and others admitted having taken part in robberies. Still another—unaware of his companion selves and obviously bewildered—had been in control when the police took Billy Milligan into custody. As Turner and other experts later testified, each of Milligan's personalities could tell right from wrong—the classic legal criterion of sanity. But all of the selves put together did not add up to a whole person who could be held legally accountable. Billy Milligan, his lawyers and psychiatrists argued, was innocent of any wrongdoing, because no single personality was responsible for his body's actions.

In a verdict without precedent in American law, Judge Jay C. Flowers agreed. On December 4, 1978, William Milligan became the first American acquitted of major criminal charges on the grounds of multiple personality. And like many defendants deemed mentally incompetent, he was then committed to the state mental-health system for an indefinite term of treatment.

Along with Milligan, according to the psychologist and four psychiatrists who gave evidence in his defense, went a stunning variety of other selves. Arthur, a scholarly Briton who had been one of the first personalities to discover he was not alone, was the stage manager of the show, deciding which self should emerge at any given time. An avid reader, he was also one of the few Milligan personalities to require glasses. Ragen, a Yugoslav mu-

nitions specialist who could speak and write the Yugoslav language of Serbo-Croatian as well as English, protected the other personalities by taking control in threatening situations. A karate expert filled with hate, Ragen openly admitted to violent, even criminal behavior; his name was thought by psychiatrists to mean "rage again."

Still another ego, Tommy, was a combative teenager with a gift for Houdini-like escapes. He once wriggled out of a straitjacket in ten seconds. Three other teenage boys held a spot on the long list of selves, as did a tormented eight-year-old named David and two females: a dyslexic three-year-old and an introverted, nineteen-year-old lesbian who eventually confessed to the rapes. Nor was that the end of Milligan's astonishing cast of internal characters. Following the trial, his doctors discovered at least thirteen more.

Psychologist William James called the sense of self "the most puzzling puzzle with which psychology has to deal." Unusual mental states like that of Billy Milligan confound common-sense notions of personal identity. They also can lead to phenomena of behavior and experience stranger than anything concocted by fiction writers or reported in the annals of the paranormal.

Such exceptional cases suggest that the healthy, integrated mind is only the most familiar of several possible models. Still other remarkable minds differ from the norm by their superior abilities. Honored as creative geniuses and visionaries, such individuals

are often described as high strung and were once considered likely to crumble under the weight of their talents. Although that old association between madness and genius is now largely discredited, the minds of the gifted remain for the most part as much a mystery as those of individuals traditionally categorized as insane.

In different cultures or ages, the symptoms now ascribed to multiple personality or other mental illnesses were variously regarded as evidence of divine inspiration, demonic possession, or mediumistic trance. Hallucinations were believed to be otherworldly visions, while obsessive-compulsive behaviors were attributed to diabolic influence.

Today, most scientists who study aberrant mental functions place the blame squarely on physiological or psychological factors. Yet some echo the theories of an earlier time, suggesting that rare minds, such as those of multiple personalities, schizophrenics, and even creative geniuses, may be tapping into a universal mind, a higher reality where all objects and events are linked to all others. "It is at least possible," suggested Graham Reed, chairman of the psychology department at Toronto's York University, "that the schizophrenic symptom, as well as nirvana, unity, and so on, merely refer to the extremes of a continuum"—that all human beings may dwell along a line stretching between the egocentric individual and the selfless universal. In fact, some maverick psychiatrists have embraced the view that mental illness is not a door closed to reality as we know it but a door opening on an-

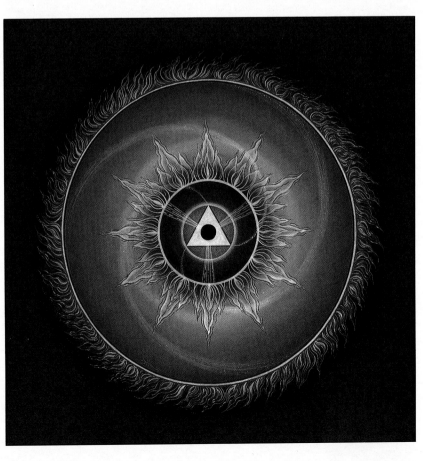

other, hidden realm. A psychosis such as schizophrenia, they believe, can be viewed as a vision quest from which much can be learned, by the therapist as well as by the sufferer.

Perhaps the most alien and alienated of human minds are those diagnosed as schizophrenic. Trapped in a world lacking meaning and in bodies seemingly beyond their control, schizophrenics account for nearly 40 percent of the admissions to state and county mental hospitals in the United States. Describing the disconnected existence of these tortured souls, medical author Patrick Young wrote that such patients "are in, but not of, the society in which they live. Their minds are divorced from reality." Their days are a cascade of tormenting delusions, hallucinations, voices, and fears.

The literal meaning of the word *schizophrenia*, which is Greek for "splitting of the mind," gives rise to a traditional, but misleading, definition of the disease as "split personality." In reality, the personality of a schizophrenic is not so much split as absent. Especially in the early stages, a patient appears flat and emotionless, devoid of feeling. Psychiatrist Edwin Fuller Torrey of Saint Elizabeth's Hospital in Washington, D.C., described two of his emotionally blank schizophrenic patients as "polite, at times stubborn, but never happy or sad." Likening their actions to those of robots, he revealed how one patient had "set fire to his house and then sat down placidly to watch TV. When it was called to his attention that the house was on fire, he got up calmly and went outside."

The accounts that schizophrenics offer of their mental ordeals further illustrate this lack of personal identity. Asked one day how he was feeling, a patient replied, "It doesn't feel. He is existing among everything. Their head is sort of swimming." Such blurred self-images make it impossible for most schizophrenics to draw a human figure on paper or to imagine or daydream. Many report feeling like puppets under someone else's control. Schizophrenics also suffer from gaps in mental logic, sometimes described as a loosening of the links between thoughts. Cause and effect, subject and object, and other logical connections fail to mesh in the schizophrenic's splintered mind. What may appear instead is something psychiatrists call word salad. An example of one patient's tumbled thought processes, as recorded in his diary, appeared in a classic 1964 study of mental illness: "When you wish upon a star Red—stop amber—caution purple—be on look out Green—go ahead with what you are doing God help us to take advice from other people and show them we can take being talked about and not get mad or lose you temper."

Perhaps the most painful syndrome of the disease is paranoid schizophrenia. The mind of a paranoid schizophrenic is a tangle of terrors. He or she hallucinates, hears threatening voices, and fears mysterious, unseen enemies. A paranoid's phantom demons usually speak aloud rather than appearing as visions, and they rarely if ever go away.

"Almost every day and every hour I hear voices about me," a 1907 case study quotes one patient as saying, "sometimes sounding from the wind, sometimes from footsteps, sometimes rattling dishes, from the rustling trees or from the wheels of passing trains."

Despite decades of research, the causes of schizophrenia remain a mystery. In the 1940s and early 1950s, European psychiatrists argued that the condition had an organic, or physical, cause within the brain. During the same period in the United States, a popular theory laid the blame instead on inadequate parents—so-called schizophrenogenic mothers who were either overprotective or rejecting, and fathers who were either too passive or too harsh.

Such psychosocial theories about schizophrenia were dealt a serious and perhaps fatal blow in the mid-1950s, however, when research at Saint Anne's Mental Hospital in Paris revealed that chlorpromazine, a drug that lowers the level of a brain chemical called dopamine, could reduce schizophrenic symptoms. To many, this suggested that the disease had a physical origin after all. More recently, investigators have discovered that the limbic system, the part of the brain responsible for emotions, is typically smaller in schizophrenics and that the cells of a schizophrenic's hippocampus—a part of the limbic system—are often seriously disorganized. Other studies have found that in many schizophrenic patients, the cavities filled with cerebrospinal fluid surrounding the brain are unusually large, indicating a smaller brain mass.

Further support for a physical cause comes from studies showing that one of ten children with a schizophrenic parent develops the disease; if both parents are afflicted, nearly half the children will become schizophrenic. Yet many

researchers believe that heredity is only part of the explanation. "It might be a virus, an autoimmune disease, an inherited defect, prenatal damage, a neurotoxin, or a multitude of things," ventures psychiatrist Daniel Weinberger of the National Institute of Mental Health, near Washington, D.C. "I don't think there's just one cause."

Despite the modern focus on the medical causes of schizophrenia, some researchers still believe that social stresses may precipitate its onset. From his completion of

By drilling holes in the skull (left), a procedure known as trepanning, medieval physicians hoped to relieve pressure on the brain and cure certain forms of madness. Surprisingly, the patients often survived. By the seventeenth century, alchemical methods were used as therapy for mental illness; in the artist's spoof above, symbols of madness go up in smoke when a patient thrusts his head into an alchemist's furnace. In the nineteenth century, electricity was touted as a panacea. With the apparatus at right, nerve specialist Jean-Martin Charcot subjected 300 patients a day to mild electrical voltages—presaging the severe shock treatments of our own era.

psychoanalytic training in 1957 until his death in 1989, the well-known Scottish psychiatrist Ronald David Laing contended that schizophrenic patients are simply trying to escape from intolerable social or family pressures. In a famous aphorism, he described schizophrenia as a sane reaction to an insane world. An individual becomes schizophrenic, Laing wrote, when he "has come to feel he is in an untenable situation. He cannot make a move, or make no move, without being beset by contradictory and paradoxical pressures and demands, pushes and pulls. . . . He is, as it were, in a position of checkmate."

Laing and other writers have speculated that schizophrenia itself—in particular, the separation from the self or ego—may enable sufferers to enter a deeper emotional reality, an inner realm of experience from which others are barred. Describing untreated schizophrenia as a hazardous but potentially educational journey into "the infinite reaches of inner space," Laing contended that common treatments meant to disrupt the normal course of the disease, such as medication and electroshock therapy, may actually prevent the voyager from returning to the outer world.

As an alternative to the medical establishment's often ineffective remedies, Laing in 1965 established the first of several healing centers for the disease. In early 1991, one center in Littleton, New Hampshire, and a number of others in the United Kingdom remained active. There, doctors and schizophrenics lived together as equals, following the same rules. "You could call them sanctuaries, like bird sanctuar-

A poet and practicing psychotherapist with an interest in
yoga, former military psychiatrist Ronald David Laing (left)
argued that schizophrenics
could be helped more by a
"caring" atmosphere and respect than by psychoactive
drugs or other invasive thera-
pies. Laing's techniques remain
in use at several treatment
centers, including Burch House
(above) in New Hampshire.

ies, for human wildlife," Laing recalled in 1988. "The half-way house idea has become embedded in the thinking of most countries, but this was a wholeway house."

The elusive self that fuzzes out of focus in schizophrenia splinters into several distinct personas in the puzzling phenomenon of multiple personality disorder—MPD, for short. A relatively rare mental condition—cases in the United States number only in the hundreds—MPD became familiar to the public at large through such popular nonfiction accounts as *The Three Faces of Eve,* published in 1957; *Sybil,* released in 1973; and news coverage of the more recent case of Billy Milligan.

Those suffering from multiple personality disorder carry within them a variety of selves, each with distinct skills, vocabularies, handwriting, and even identifiable differences in appearance. The range of behavioral and physical variations in the personalities can be astonishing. Sometimes one self can drive while the others cannot. One may be nearsighted or color-blind, yet others will have normal vision. A woman named Marion told Judith Hooper and Dick Teresi, authors of a 1988 book entitled *The Three-Pound Universe,* that she had sung in three different sections of the chorus at her high school in western Massachusetts—alto, second soprano, and first tenor.

Some multiples, as MPD sufferers are informally known, contend there are advantages to their condition; one valiantly described it as "a unique and wonderful defense mechanism that not everyone can have." But the phenomenon is typically found in people who report having suffered horrific abuse as children. According to most therapists, the different selves they developed helped the youngsters cope with unspeakable experiences and fears that often continued throughout their teenage years.

Billy Milligan, for instance, claimed to have been buried alive at the age of fourteen by his stepfather, with only a pipe to breathe through. Then, according to Milligan, his stepfather—who heatedly denied the entire story—urinated into the pipe. During such episodes, the boy learned to shut his eyes and "go away," he says, returning to awareness

days or even years later with no memory of the intervening time. Psychiatrists suggest the process of developing multiple personalities is a gradual one. Each time a child enters a self-induced trance, they say, the "trance-state consciousness"—or new self—becomes more autonomous. Friends or family members may not even realize when someone close to them has developed MPD; the person may simply seem moody or forgetful.

One of the first reputable scientists to explore the phenomenon was the pioneering psychologist William James. James's interest in the disorder began in the late 1880s, when he became involved in the sensational case of Ansel

As psychotherapist David Goldblatt (standing) readies a fish for cooking, a convivial group of staff members and clients—a term used in preference to "patients"—gather around the kitchen table at Burch House in 1991. In the letter at right, a former resident gratefully wrote to a therapist, "When I came to Burch House, I was diagnosed as being a Human Being."

DEAR KATY,

It has been almost two years since I saw you last at Burch House.

During my life I've been diagnosed as a "Functional Psychotic", "Manic Depressive", "Delayed stress syndrome", "Schizo", and "mystic with psychotic features", ect. (Depending on what I looked like at the time.)

When I came to Burch House I was diagnosed as being a <u>Human Being</u> and accepted as part of the Burch House Family. This is what made all the difference for me. Working with other people there was also very important for a loner like me. I didn't feel as isolated, the insights I gained have been effective in my life and Art therapy studies.

So I want to thank you again for your work and for making Burch House possible.

Sincerely
Tony ——

Bourne, a sixty-one-year-old itinerant preacher from Greene, Rhode Island. Bourne withdrew $551 from his bank account one day in January 1887, boarded a horsecar, and vanished without a trace. Two months later, hundreds of miles away, a shopkeeper known to his neighbors as A. J. Brown awoke in a house in Norristown, Pennsylvania, and demanded to know where he was and how he got there. His name, he said, was the Reverend Ansel Bourne.

Bourne, by his own account, had no recollection of traveling to Norristown, nor of renting the shop from which he sold fruit, stationery, and confections. The last thing he remembered was withdrawing money from the Rhode Island bank. Understandably concerned, Bourne allowed James to hypnotize him to see if the shopkeeper personality would appear. Indeed, when the minister fell under the hypnotic spell, he promptly became Brown again. He failed to recognize his own wife—that is, Bourne's wife—and could recall every detail of his sojourn in Norristown.

A frustrated James was unable to fuse the two personalities under hypnosis as he had hoped to do. He could only conclude that Bourne had somehow experienced a spontaneous hypnotic trance on the January day he disappeared, and he had taken on a new identity. "The peculiarity," James later commented, "is that nothing else like it ever occurred in the man's life, and that no eccentricity of character came out." Struck by that and other oddities about Bourne's story, subsequent medical historians have questioned whether the case was indeed one of true multiple personality or simply garden-variety amnesia brought on by Bourne's wish to escape his old life in Greene.

No such questions surround the subsequent case of Christine Beauchamp. A frail, nervous young woman, Beauchamp turned up at the Boston office of psychologist Morton Prince one day in 1898, suffering from what Prince later described as "inhibition of will" and a symptom known as ataxia—uncontrollable, jerky body movements.

When Prince began his treatment by putting Beauchamp into a deep hypnotic trance, he was startled to

meet with two more personalities. The first was a relaxed version of Christine, whom Prince dubbed B-2. The other personality, who called herself Sally, was unlike Christine in every way. Sally derided Christine as "prissy" and liked to shock her host by having her regain awareness with her feet propped on a table and a wineglass in her hand. More cruelly, Sally once terrified Christine by planting the idea in her head that both her feet had been amputated.

As the sessions progressed, a fourth personality emerged, this one relatively mature and self-controlled. Prince gave her the prosaic name B-4. According to the psychologist, Sally and B-4 seemed to vie for Christine's attention. When Christine took a train to New York to look for work, for instance, Sally got off at New Haven and impulsively took a job as a waitress; B-4 quit the job and went back to Boston.

Prince gradually pieced together Christine's story. Her mother had died when she was thirteen, and her alcoholic father proved a destructive and unreliable caretaker. Christine endured psychologically intact until one day when a family friend—someone she thought of as a kindly father figure—tried to give her a none-too-paternal kiss. At that moment, according to Prince, the young woman's identity disintegrated and the alternate selves appeared.

Prince decided to "exorcise" the troublesome Sally under hypnosis and then blend together Christine, B-2, and B-4—a plan that would be frowned upon by most modern specialists, who believe that all the selves must be brought together for a permanent recovery. Sally herself initially balked at Prince's plan but eventually seemed to capitulate, and Christine's personality stabilized. But the cure, as Prince reported several years later, was only partially successful. Sally continued to make rare cameo appearances, usually to play a practical joke on Christine.

In France, the prominent psychiatrist Pierre Janet attended a case similar to Christine Beauchamp's. It involved a forty-five-year-old Frenchwoman named Leonie, who visited the doctor complaining of hysteria and sleepwalking, two conditions that had tormented her since childhood.

Janet hypnotized her, and two personalities quite unlike Leonie's waking self were revealed to the doctor. The first, whom Janet called Leonie 2, was cheerful, noisy, uninhibited—and quite scornful of Leonie 1. "That good woman is not myself," Leonie 2 asserted, "she is too stupid." When a sober and slow-speaking Leonie 3 materialized, she disdained both the others. Leonie 1 was too dense, she told Janet, and Leonie 2 was a "crazy creature." In later discussions of the case, Janet attributed Leonie's three selves not to the kind of childhood trauma suggested by modern theory but to the projection of unconscious wishes by Leonie 1, whom he considered the core personality.

The Leonie case and others like it fascinated one of Janet's students in psychiatry, Carl Jung. Eager to explore the disorder in detail, Jung wrote his doctoral dissertation, published in 1902, on the multiple lives of his fifteen-year-old cousin, Helene Preiswerk. Ordinarily a shy, uneducated girl, Preiswerk sometimes metamorphosed into an assured, assertive, and literate woman who spoke High German instead of her native Swiss German—so different a dialect as to be almost a separate language. On still other occasions she assumed the mannerisms of a nobleman, a bantering flirt, and even her deceased clergyman grandfather.

Preiswerk believed herself to be a medium, and several of her alternate personalities claimed to be spirits—theories Jung dismissed in favor of psychoanalytic explanations. In the course of his research, Jung attended several séances conducted by his cousin. Guests would join hands around a table, and when the table began to move, Preiswerk would enter a trance during which spirits could speak through her. The most articulate of these was a woman named Ivenes, who claimed that in earlier lives she had been a Christian martyr and a countess burned as a witch.

In his dissertation, Jung concluded that his cousin's various incarnations personified unconscious and incomplete parts of herself with the power to take temporary control of her body. This analysis led in turn to a major principle of Jungian psychoanalysis, the idea that mental illness reflects a splintering or disunity in the personality. A healthy personality, Jung wrote, is an integrated whole that merges the conscious and the unconscious minds.

Interest in multiple personality disorder declined during the early decades of the 1900s. Although MPD cases continued to be reported in the psychiatric literature, the diagnosis remained controversial. Many doctors regarded apparent multiple personalities as theatrical displays subconsciously created by a strong, central ego. It was not until the publication in 1957 of The Three Faces of Eve that interest in the disorder revived. Written by Corbett Thigpen and Hervey Cleckley, who had treated a woman with three personalities, the book described in harrowing detail how hypnotic therapy had uncovered Eve's repressed memories of the childhood abuses that had fractured her core self.

Later made into an Oscar-winning film, the popular case study told only part of the fascinating story. In a 1976 work titled I'm Eve, the woman portrayed in the earlier book not only revealed her true identity as Chris Sizemore, a California homemaker, but described how the earlier therapy had failed when additional selves, holding still more secret memories, had emerged. According to Sizemore, her real recovery began almost two decades after the initial attempt, when a new team of therapists gradually elicited nineteen more personalities. In the sessions that followed, her many selves were at last able to identify the scope of their illness and the tragedies of their shared past. After intensive negotiations among the personalities, they merged into a singular self who described their ordeal in I'm Eve and its 1988 sequel, A Mind of My Own.

That Eve eventually exhibited more than twenty different personalities was not in itself exceptional, as proved by a number of subsequent cases, including that of a young woman known by the pseudonym Sybil Dorsett. The story of Sybil unfolded in a book of the same name, written by Flora Rheta Schreiber, a former editor of Science Digest. According to Schreiber, who interviewed Dorsett and her psychiatrist, Cornelia Wilbur, over a period of several years, Dorsett's personality began to fracture in the 1930s as a

very young child growing up in New England. Eventually, she developed sixteen strikingly varied selves, including a talented writer-painter, a musician, a cheerful teenager, and a two-year-old girl. Each displayed such distinctive behavior that Dr. Wilbur said she could tell from a glimpse of Sybil in the waiting room which personality was in control.

Using hypnosis, still the most common form of treatment for MPD, Dr. Wilbur eventually learned of the sadistic atrocities that Dorsett had suffered at the hands of her mentally ill mother. With each successive shock, the child had fled into another self. Although therapy was complicated by Dorsett's reluctance to blame her mother—the sessions continued for more than ten years—the young woman was eventually restored to a single, whole individual.

That happy ending was equally elusive for Billy Milligan, the young Ohio man arrested for rape in 1977. Although an account of his case published in 1981 details two periods around the time of Milligan's trial during which his personalities began to fuse, the process was later reversed. Apparently the stress of intense press coverage and his transfer to a more restrictive hospital in Dayton caused an agonizing breakup of his fragile core ego. Several of his alternate selves assumed joint control, and on July 4, 1986, the personality known as Tommy engineered a successful escape from the hospital. Milligan became the subject of a national manhunt and was traced by the FBI to Colorado, Washington, and finally to southern Florida, where he was recaptured five months after his flight.

Returned to Ohio and committed to a mental hospital in Columbus, Milligan en-

Nineteenth-century American psychologist William James (below) speculated that multiple personalities are formed when "weak" patients relinquish parts of their consciousness. The fragments, he wrote, "may solidify into a secondary subconscious self."

dured another two years in a seemingly hopeless depression. That despair apparently led to the young man's recovery, however: In an attempt to save Milligan from his bleak situation, the various selves decided to fuse once again. On May 2, 1988, an Ohio judge released Milligan from custody, declaring that his many personalities had "welded together." Gainfully employed since that time as a computer programmer and freelance artist, Milligan remained a ward of the court as of early 1991.

Despite the well-publicized cases of Eve and Sybil, and the legal recognition of Billy Milligan's multiple selves, the disorder continued to be a somewhat suspect diagnosis for many psychiatrists to accept until the early 1980s, when experiments conducted by Dr. Frank Putnam at the National Institute of Mental Health gave scientific support to the subjective experience of multiple personality. Putnam, a psychiatrist, had treated his first multiple—a woman misdiagnosed as clinically depressed—in 1979; over the next few years he handled 150 more cases. Intrigued by the apparent prevalence of what was considered a rare disorder, Putnam undertook a series of groundbreaking neurological studies of the disease. In one 1982 experiment, he compared the brain waves of professional actors portraying different characters with those of ten MPD patients slipping in and out of their various identities. Although both the actors and the patients outwardly appeared to change their personalities, he found that the brain-wave patterns of the actors remained relatively constant from one character to the next, while those of the patients suffering from multiple personality disorder changed

Scribbled, printed, or carefully inscribed, the markedly different writing samples below represent only a few of the ninety-two personalities sharing the body of Truddi Chase. Before Chase became aware of her condition, still another personality retyped such manuscripts in order to conceal the variations in her handwriting.

Differing by 99.7 percent according to a standard comparison, the so-called brain maps at left—which use shape and color to display brain-wave pattern and amplitude—reflect two selves of a woman with multiple personality disorder. In the top map, light blue tones reveal that a matronly personality, known as Rachael, generates relatively strong delta waves. Black and purple shades in the lower map indicate that the delta waves are faint or absent in the scan of her angry and suicidal basic self, "S."

radically as the alternate personalities took control.

In a follow-up study, Putnam found that blood-flow patterns in the brain also fluctuated as individuals moved from one identity to another, and a colleague of Putnam's discovered measurable differences in the voiceprints of separate personalities. The conclusion was remarkable: Just as the behaviors of various selves were unique to each individual, so too were their brain functions. Multiple personality disorder had been put on a firm scientific footing—almost a century after psychiatrists had first observed it.

That result would not have come as a surprise to the authors of an extraordinary book titled *When Rabbit Howls,* published in 1987. Written by the ninety-two selves who inhabit a woman known as Truddi Chase, the book presents a set of personalities who have chosen to remain divided. According to the personalities, who call themselves the Troops, the original Truddi Chase "went to sleep" when she was raped at the age of two and has never reawakened. Although that self did not die, they say, she also never grew up, remaining as innocent and inexperienced as any two-year-old child. As suggested by their joint authorship of the book, the selves inside Truddi Chase function effectively as a team, working a responsible but unidentified job as they make a type of communal life for themselves. Some remain articulate and adult, others wounded and childlike. The personality closest to the lost two-year-old self is known as Rabbit. Incapable of speech or writing, Rabbit—for whom the book is named—expresses the child's stored pain with an animal's anguished howls.

The public had a glimpse of the practical implications of such a complicated existence in November 1990, when a woman known only as Sarah unveiled six of her forty-six personalities during her testimony in a Wisconsin criminal case. Age twenty-seven at the time of the trial, Sarah, a trim Korean-American raised in Iowa, accused twenty-nine-year-old Mark Peterson of taking advantage of one of her less responsible selves—alleging, in legal terms, that he had knowingly had sex with a person "mentally unable to assess her conduct." For his part, Peterson admitted the sexual encounter but denied knowing at the time that Sarah was mentally ill.

On the witness stand, Sarah and her various selves provided compelling testimony. "Who would be in the best position to talk about that night?" prosecutor Joseph Paulus asked Sarah in a widely reported exchange.

"Franny," she replied.

"Would it be possible for us to meet Franny, and talk to her?"

"Yes," Sarah said. "Now?"

Without further ado, she dropped her chin, sat motionless for about five seconds, then looked straight at the prosecutor and murmured "Hel-lo." Franny had arrived.

Quickly sworn in by Judge Robert Hawley, Franny testified that she had met Peterson and that during their conversation had told him about her various identities. Later, she said, he asked to meet "the one who likes to have fun"—the self named Jennifer. "I went away," Franny recounted, and the childishly innocent Jennifer appeared. Following the thread of the story, the prosecutor then asked whether Jennifer could testify. In response, the witness closed her eyes and dipped her head again, then blinked and asked for a drink of water in a high-pitched voice.

After taking a sworn oath, Jennifer airily described her date with Peterson. She removed her shorts, she explained, "because he told me to." Asked if she objected to sex, she replied, "Tell me what sex is and I'll tell you if I objected." As the extraordinary testimony unfolded, the prosecutor summoned and questioned three more personalities—a six-year-old named Emily, a woman named Leslie, and an animal-like character named Sam who growled when he was afraid. Although Leslie and Sam had little to contribute, Emily testified that she had seen the sexual encounter, candidly confessing, "I was peeking the whole time." The day in court ended abruptly when Jennifer reappeared to announce she was hungry and wanted to go home.

On the basis of the personalities' testimonies, Peterson was convicted of the assault charge, but the verdict was

Painted after three years of psychoanalysis, this 1957 self-portrait by the multiple-personality sufferer known as Sybil employs blue watercolors to merge three women into one. Blue was Sybil's favorite color; she once said it represented all the shades of love.

later overturned because defense attorneys had been unable to conduct a pretrial psychiatric examination of Sarah. The state subsequently decided against a retrial to avoid subjecting the fragile young woman to further distress.

Uncanny enough in its own right, multiple personality disorder has also been repeatedly linked to paranormal phenomena. Certain researchers, for instance, believe that not all the selves manifested by a multiple are internally generated. Some, they venture, may be spirits from another realm, or as one therapist suggested, the vestiges of past lives. In the 1980s, American psychiatrist Ralph Allison coined the term Inner Self Helper to describe a special entity that helps the patient to heal and reintegrate. Personalities of this type often claim to be conduits for divine love and healing power, and Allison suggests they may in fact enter the patient from an out-

side beneficent power. "There is always a logical reason for the alter personality's existence," Allison believes. "Thus the discovery of an entity who doesn't serve any recognizable purpose presents a diagnostic problem. Such entities often refer to themselves as spirits. Over the years I've encountered too many such cases to dismiss the possibility of spirit possession completely."

Truddi Chase, for example, counts among her ninety-two personalities one named Ean, who has a rich brogue and a vivid memory of a past life in Ireland. Wise and well balanced, he looks after the other selves. "Who is Ean, really?" wrote Chase's psychologist, Robert Phillips, in an afterword to *When Rabbit Howls*. "He seems to be part of the Troops—yet also is separate from them. It is said that Ean sits 'above.' He works powerfully behind the scenes, and he emanates great energy. It is also said of him that he is not only of this time but also timeless."

An equally mysterious Inner Self Helper became a key factor in the recovery of multiple personality sufferer Kit—short for Katherine—Castle. As chronicled by author Stefan Bechtel in the 1989 book *Katherine, It's Time*, Castle began undergoing treatment for MPD in New York State in the 1980s. As with many other multiples, therapy revealed that her core self had begun to shatter during childhood. Among her resident personalities, Castle apparently hosted a guardian angel named Michael, who was described by various selves who had seen and heard him as a kindly man in a dark hat and coat. Michael first appeared on the day that a family friend who had provided emotional support for the young Kit died before her eyes, killed in a stock-car racing crash.

Many years later, explains Bechtel, a personality called Me-Liz saw

William "Billy" Milligan smiles shyly in a snapshot (below) taken in 1981 at a maximum-security psychiatric hospital. By then his gentle demeanor hid twenty-three distinct personalities—some mature, some criminal, and some childishly sweet. Allen, one of several artists among them, drew and painted these portraits of six of the other personalities. Fourth from the left is Adalana, a young woman who was the only personality implicated in the rapes that occasioned Milligan's commitment to the Ohio state mental-health system in 1978.

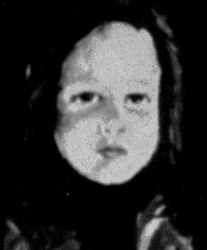

Arthur, Milligan's most responsible personality, spoke with a British accent, read and wrote Arabic, and enjoyed medical books. Distant, unemotional, and extremely intelligent, he arbitrated disputes among the other personalities.

Four years old, deaf, and possibly retarded, Shawn was one of thirteen suppressed selves that Arthur considered "undesirable." On rare occasions, Shawn emerged anyway, making a buzzing sound so that he could feel the vibration in his head.

Three-year-old Christine, shown clutching her favorite rag doll, was an intelligent little girl with dyslexia who liked to draw butterflies and flowers. In a note to Milligan's attorney Judy Stevenson, this personality once asked why she had to stay "in a cage" when she wanted to go out and play.

Michael on a Virginia seashore, "absurdly overdressed in the heat, wearing a dark coat, dark trousers, and holding a dark hat in his hands." He was not alone. "Behind and above him, hanging in the air like three flashing, ghostly cymbals, were the beings." According to Me-Liz, Michael had told Castle to expect these ghostly visitations, "that they would signify a great new unfolding in her life. Something grand and wonderful was preparing to take place."

As therapy progressed, Michael and the beings of light who accompanied him acted as partners in the process of healing, convincing Castle's selves to fuse into one. The process came to its logical climax in what Castle now refers to as the "final farandola," an intense, all but indescribable experience of bright lights and a whirling sensation supervised by Michael; Castle emerged from the event alone.

Views on Michael's identity, and that of other Inner Self Helpers, vary. Psychiatrist Cornelia Wilbur, who helped treat Castle, suggests that Michael was simply a projection or mental image. "Being able to visualize the Inner Self Helper is a way of preserving its integrity, its separateness,"

Wilbur has commented. "It's a way of saying, 'This has nothing to do with me, it is someone completely outside of me, helping me.'" On the other hand, Kit Castle's minister, Kaye DeYoung, is equally convinced that Michael was indeed a separate being. "I considered Michael to be an angel. I believe in angels," he wrote. "I know God speaks, and he speaks to people in different ways." For his part, Joseph Pearce, author of *The Crack in the Cosmic Egg*, has compared the Inner Self Helper to the Buddhist concept of the *tulpa*, a phantasmic spirit-self that passes on from one generation to the next. Usually hidden from the conscious persona, the protective being sometimes emerges during the rigorous training undergone by Tibetan monks.

Whatever the origin of their various selves, people with multiple personality disorder seem exceptionally open to paranormal events of many kinds. Chris Sizemore, the original "Eve," for example, repeatedly experienced what she described as precognitive visions. She alleged that on one occasion she convinced her husband to stay home because of a fear he would be electrocuted; a co-worker who

Beautiful as a Renaissance Madonna, nineteen-year-old Adalana was a lesbian who yearned for love and intimacy—urges that allegedly caused her to commit three rapes using Milligan's body. Unlike any of the other personalities, she suffered from nystagmus, a medical condition in which the eyes involuntarily dart back and forth.

The first self to reveal Milligan's multiple personality disorder, eight-year-old David endured pain and suffering for all of the alter egos. Perhaps as a result, he was often confused and had a short attention span. This is a detail from David's portrait; Allen painted him small, in one corner of an otherwise featureless canvas, suggesting the isolation of an abused child.

Nineteen years old, with a Boston accent, April was regarded by the other selves as insane because of her violent plans for revenge against the man she believed abused Billy Milligan as a child. Despite her differences with the others, she helped with sewing and other housework.

According to Kit Castle, a woman who recovered from multiple personality disorder in 1986, hazy lights always appeared in photographs of her "Me-Liz" personality—including the one above, taken at a party. An alleged psychic, Me-Liz was one of several Castle personalities who reported encounters with a guardian angel named Michael, depicted in a sketch by Castle at right. A compassionate figure who comforted Castle as a child, Michael claimed to come from her "real father" in the sky. "When you turn on the porch light in your heart," the little girl heard him say, "He'll send me to help you."

took his place that day was indeed electrocuted on the job. Similarly, Billy Milligan's family reportedly was accustomed to the fact that Billy seemed to sense when his sister was in trouble, even when she was hundreds of miles away.

By some accounts, multiple personalities also seem to generate or absorb vast amounts of energy, physical and psychic. Psychiatrist Ralph Allison has remarked on being psychically sapped of vitality by a woman patient with multiple personalities. Truddi Chase's therapist, Robert Phillips, experienced just the opposite effect, feeling abnormally well and energetic after each meeting with her. Yet in *When Rabbit Howls,* Chase's personalities report a persistent problem with light bulbs and car batteries—left in their vicinity, say the selves, both items very soon go dead. On an even more dramatic note, a nineteenth-century source tells of an apparent multiple named Mollie Fancher—also known as the Brooklyn Enigma—who was said to kill small pets by draining their life force.

Psychic researcher Scott Rogo reported that he asked Ralph Allison how many of those afflicted with MPD seem to have paranormal abilities. "Every one of them," the psychiatrist responded. "It may be the primary personality that has some ability to tell what's coming up in the future for her kids, or accidents they're going to get into. That happens quite frequently. . . . If the patient has a lot of personalities, there will be one who is very psychic, and the others will have average ability or no abilities."

In addition to their supposed psychic powers, people with MPD tend to be unusually creative, typically harboring musicians, painters, and authors among their many egos. But the condition itself is perhaps the ultimate creative answer to unbearable reality. In the face of childhood anguish, those with multiple personalities did not retreat into psychosis. Instead, each invented new selves to share the horror in a painful but necessary triumph over tragedy.

The idea of a link between creativity and mental instability is certainly nothing new. "The lunatic, the lover and the poet," Shakespeare wrote in *A Midsummer Night's Dream,* "are of imagination all compact." A generation later, the poet John Dryden agreed. "Great wits are sure to madness near allied," he wrote, "and thin partitions do their bounds divide." For his part, the French author Marcel Proust stated flatly that "everything great comes from neurotics," among whom he evidently included himself. "They alone," he said, "have founded religions and composed our masterpieces."

By the nineteenth century, the link between genius and insanity was accepted scientific dogma. French psychiatrist Moreau de Tours contended that both states stemmed from mental overactivity. Cesare Lombroso, an Italian physician and early criminologist, saw genius as a psychosis related to epilepsy. And in the 1890s a British doctor named John Nisbet concluded that genius and madness were simply different phases of a "morbid susceptibility" that resulted from an imbalance in the cerebrospinal system.

William James, however, strongly disagreed. There was no accepted definition of genius, he declared, and no evidence that insanity was more common among the brilliant and accomplished. In the end, statistical surveys bore him out; mental illness occurs as commonly in the population as a whole as it does among the gifted few. Yet the roll call of great minds clouded by mental illness is a long one, an extraordinary compendium of struggles waged simultaneously against inner demons and real-world adversity. The great seventeenth-century mathematician and physicist Isaac Newton, for instance, fell victim at the age of fifty to a paranoid breakdown that incapacitated him for a year and a half. Chronically absent-minded and quarrelsome, Newton had trouble eating and sleeping for several months prior to the episode. He accused friends of conspiring against him and claimed to hear conversations no one else could. One reputable biographer has since speculated that Newton, a lifelong bachelor who showed little interest in women, lost his mental bearings because of suppressed homosexual impulses. Psychiatrist and author Anthony Storr suggests instead that Newton's midlife paranoia stemmed from the effects of his having been aban-

doned by his mother when he was a three-year-old child.

Another Englishman, the brilliant eighteenth-century writer and scholar Samuel Johnson, was prey to such black depressions that he once instructed his housekeeper to lock him in his room and place him in chains if he became demented. Johnson also practiced various obsessive-compulsive rituals. On passing through a doorway, reported a woman friend, he "would give a sudden spring and make such an extensive stride as if trying for a wager how far he could stride." He also stepped over cracks in paving stones and touched every pole when walking along a road.

More than a century later, Winston Churchill, the prime minister of England during World War II, found himself at the mercy of what he called his "black dog"—abject depressions. As a child, Churchill was shunted from one boarding school to another by a socialite mother and politician father who had scant time for him. His letters home were pathetic pleas for visits and mail he rarely received. Psychiatrist Storr believes that Churchill grew up convinced that only by doing exceptional things could he earn the love and respect he craved; his ferocious energy, according to Storr, was fueled by the fear that despair would overtake him if he stopped to rest. In slack periods, Churchill sank into a melancholy that he escaped only intermittently through writing and painting; late in his life, the once-dynamic wartime leader and eloquent orator sat alone for hours at a time in what amounted to a depressive stupor. "I have achieved a great deal," he said to his daughter Diana, "to achieve nothing in the end."

Although individual examples such as Newton, Johnson, and Churchill cannot outweigh the statistics showing no consistent link between madness and genius, a few scientists wonder if the two mental conditions may stem from a similar source. Research has shown, writes psychiatrist Storr, that "some psychological characteristics which are inherited as part of the predisposition to schizophrenia are divergent, loosely associative styles of thinking which, when normal, are 'creative.'" Similarly,

Author Mary Shelley (above), the creator of Victor Frankenstein and his monster (right), wrote that the enduring story "sprang from a waking dream of extraordinary vividness"—said by many to be a common source of creativity. Shelley's vision blended horror with a recent discovery: that electricity could make dead frog legs twitch as though restoring them to life.

psychiatrist Roland Fischer of Washington, D.C.'s Georgetown University believes that the hallucinations that are symptoms of madness in some people are mystical founts of creativity in others. He calls such experiences "communications with the unknown."

The father of psychoanalysis himself, Sigmund Freud, struggled to explain the roots of creativity. "Analysis," he once confessed, "can do nothing toward elucidating the nature of the artistic gift, nor can it explain the means by which the artist works." He concluded that artists are simply better than most people at channeling fantasies into something useful. But since, in Freud's view, fantasy is an unhealthy escape from reality—"a happy person never fantasizes"—artists are by his definition unhappy and unhealthy.

Asked to supply their own explanation of the creative process, poets, musicians, and other artists often ascribe inspiration to a power outside themselves. Just as the Greeks spoke of the muses—the nine goddesses of the arts—John Milton wrote of a "celestial patroness" who dictated to him what he modestly called "my unprecedented verse." British Romantic poet Percy Bysshe Shelley seems to have shared a similar experience. "A man cannot say, 'I will compose poetry,'" he wrote, "for the mind in creation is as a fading coal, which some invisible influence, like an inconstant wind, awakens to transitory brightness."

William Thackeray, the author of *Vanity Fair* and other popular nineteenth-century works, remarked that it sometimes seemed "as if an occult power was moving the pen." The character, he said, "does or says something and I ask, how the dickens did he come to think of that?" Similarly, the novelist Mary Ann Evans, who wrote under the pseu-

The manuscript below, a minuet composed and transcribed by Wolfgang Amadeus Mozart at the tender age of four, is evidence of his remarkable genius. Here pictured seated at the keyboard at six years old, Mozart said he received his compositions "complete and finished" in his mind.

donym George Eliot, said that in her best writing she felt that her personality became a mere instrument for a "spirit" that took possession of her.

Such descriptions of creative automatism abound in the world of music as well. The precocious eighteenth-century genius Wolfgang Amadeus Mozart declared in an oft-quoted letter that he heard compositions in his head before he wrote them down. They arrived almost fully formed, he said. "Nor do I hear in my imagination the parts successively, but I hear them, as it were, all at once." To occupy his conscious mind while he transmitted the sounds to paper, Mozart sometimes asked his wife, Constanze, to read to him as he composed. Four generations later, the Russian composer Peter Ilyich Tchaikovsky paid his own tribute to a subconscious inner force. When in the throes of creation, he said, "I forget everything and behave like a madman. Everything within me starts pulsing and quivering."

The same ungovernable force also seems to affect

those who perform music. To describe her most intense state of artistic immersion and creativity, concert violinist Nadja Salerno-Sonnenberg refers to "the zone," a phrase athletes often use to identify the consciousness level that leads to peak performance. The zone, she says, is "a heightened feeling where everything is right. Everything comes together. Everything is one. Everybody agrees. Everybody is with you and you, yourself, are not battling yourself. It's very, very rare."

Such accounts may refer, some experts believe, to a level of awareness suspended between the conscious and the unconscious. Carl Jung identified a similar mental state as the "primordial" mind; others call it reverie. In the 1960s, Harold Rugg, a researcher at Columbia University, dubbed this misty middle ground the "transliminal mind," a condition he associated not only with creativity but also with the meditative states of Eastern religions, light hypnotic trances, intuition, and hypnagogic states—those periods between sleep and wakefulness. Whatever this state is called, its chief attribute is an uncritical ambiance of relaxed readiness and receptivity. Open to any and all ideas, the transliminal mind eventually finds the simplest image or set of symbols that solve the creative problem confronting it, said Rugg. The result is a seemingly magical creative flash.

Creative artists have always had ways of courting the inspirational state. In a recipe similar to that followed by many another author, Samuel Johnson required a purring cat, an orange peel, and a cup of tea to write. Rudyard Kipling needed dark black ink; Proust labored in a soundproof room; and the Baltimorean sage H. L. Mencken washed his hands dozens of times daily. The German dramatist and poet J. C. Friedrich von Schiller was able to detect the muse in the odor of rotting apples, and he always kept some handy.

Linked by most neurologists to the right hemisphere of the brain—the province of imagination, intuition, and visual rather than verbal concepts—creativity has also been associated in some studies with theta waves, one of four general categories of brain waves. Researchers at the Menninger

Foundation in Kansas have found a resemblance between the mental images described by creative people and the vivid, sometimes mystical visions experienced by volunteers trained to produce theta waves. Other scientists have noted that theta waves are often associated with rage and violence—a modern reappearance of the old notions connecting genius and madness.

In recent years, neurologists have also identified at least one disorder apparently linked to musical talent: Tourette's syndrome, a neurological condition that begins with facial and muscular tics and progresses to uncontrollable outbursts of obscenity, imitations, and outlandish remarks. Neurologist and author Oliver Sacks treated a Tourette's patient who was a talented drummer, famous for wild riffs ignited by a tic or a compulsive rat-a-tat. Sacks found a drug that quieted the man's symptoms, at the cost of his musical virtuosity. The patient compromised, taking the medicine during the week but not on weekends.

Yet another musician, pianist-songwriter Connie Cook of Peoria, Illinois, claimed to have acquired her abilities by still another means—albeit one at which many would scoff. Cook reports that one night in 1981 she dreamed of friendly aliens from the Pleiades star cluster; a month later, she began compulsively writing songs. Before that, she says, she could not play a note, but now "music just flows out of me." She became a professional pianist, playing in a Peoria singles bar. Whatever the explanation, Cook has clearly tapped into a talent she had previously lacked. Her sister Carolyn, who rejects the UFO story, concedes that when Connie plays, "those aren't her fingers on the keys."

Although scorned by her sister, Cook's dream of an alien encounter would likely get a warmer reception from the highly creative mental minority known as fantasy-prone personalities. These are natural visionaries who live out much of their lives in one or more alternate realities of their own invention. By some accounts, they may make up as much as four percent of the population.

Fantasy-prone personalities first attracted scientific notice in the 1960s, when a Stanford University researcher,

Josephine Hilgard, began a study of good hypnotic subjects and the traits they have in common. To her surprise, Hilgard discovered that the best subjects almost always enjoyed extraordinarily vivid fantasy lives. Intrigued by that finding, Boston psychologists Theodore Barber and Sheryl Wilson interviewed another twenty-seven highly receptive hypnotic subjects. All but one had profoundly detailed imaginary existences. Many spent as much as 95 percent of their waking moments in realms of their own creation.

Further research by Ohio University psychologist Steven Jay Lynn helped profile the typical fantasy-prone personality. Evenly divided between males and females, fantasy-prone individuals represent a cross section of age and personality type. One in four, says Lynn, shows signs of mental disturbance; one in ten has trouble turning off their fantasies long enough to perform daily tasks. Yet the condition also serves a critical stabilizing role. Lynn found that fantasies "contributed to psychological well-being" by helping the individuals cope with adversity and stress.

The elaborate inner lives of the fantasy prone are of a far different order than daydreams. Fully three-quarters of the group, for instance, are able to reach sexual climax by fantasy alone. "When I 'go away' I'm very definitely there and not here," one woman explained to an *Omni* magazine reporter. "I touch other people, other things, hear them, laugh, dance, talk, cry, scream, get scared, see and know everything that's going on."

Their constant imagining apparently makes fantasy-prone people hypersensitive to drugs, emotional stress, and even popular entertainment. Movies may be indistinguishable from reality. "To me it's real," the same woman remarked. "I scream or hyperventilate. . . . When I saw *Rambo* I ended up hiding under my seat." The fantasy prone may also experience a wide range of psychic phenomena—or, perhaps, fantasies of such phenomena. In their study, Barber and Wilson found that fantasy-prone subjects often reported clairvoyant dreams, out-of-body experiences, past-life regressions, and other brushes with the paranormal.

In 1988, *Omni* magazine attempted to get an inside look at the condition by asking several fantasy-prone personalities for details of their current scenarios. Among the results was a 2,500-word epic by a woman from Oregon. Much as a movie fan might watch a videotape over and over again, searching out favorite scenes, she claimed to have run the fantasy footage over and over in her mind for several years. In short, the fantasy begins with the woman walking alone in a strange forest. She comes upon a group of people with golden skin and bright orange eyes and learns that they are slaves. A woman she befriends teaches her their language, and in the evenings she listens to eerie music played on odd-looking instruments.

Eventually, she and her friend escape to the rocky realm of the "northern people." Along the way she eats a fruit whose taste and texture she can describe to the last seed: "fleshy and very sweet," she reports, "a bit like a melon but with a slightly rancid taste." In time, they find the northerners, who have long gray hair and gray eyes and wear medieval clothes. After a stint as a potato peeler, the woman is granted an audience with the bejeweled king; his gems are "quite lovely," she adds, "but nothing extremely flashy." The king treats her kindly and offers to make her a scribe. But then she meets an alien who wants her to travel to his planet as a sort of ambassador trainee. She decides to go. And there it ends.

Although fantasy-prone personalities are usually able to harness their extraordinary imaginations, they cannot simply break the narrative habit. Like those with schizophrenia, multiple personality disorder, or even exceptional artistic talent, the fantasy prone cannot take the human mind for granted. For them, its possibilities and limitations are the stuff of ordinary life. But in the daily mental struggle, those gifted or burdened with rare minds may capture a reality that more comfortable mentalities will never see. As psychiatrist Ronald David Laing wrote in 1967, "The ego is the instrument for living in this world. If the ego is broken up or destroyed, then the person may be exposed to other worlds, 'real' in different ways."

Time Out of Mind

Individuality itself seemed to dissolve and fade away into boundless being," wrote Alfred, Lord Tennyson; "death was an almost laughable impossibility." The poet had experienced a mystical trance, a rapturous feeling that his soul had soared free of his body. It was, he affirmed, "not a confused state but the clearest, the surest of the sure, utterly beyond words." Tennyson was not alone in treasuring such an experience.

Every culture in every age has recognized and prized this exalted condition. The revered oracles of ancient Greece delivered their prophecies while in trances, and religious mystics through the ages have sought revelatory visions in the same way. The behavior of the entranced—whose gaze may seem riveted on a vision unperceived by others—demonstrate that entrancement is a kind of changed reality: in effect, an altered state of being.

The ancient adventure comes in many forms. Mind-altering drugs may induce trances, but their use can be dangerous as well as illegal. One medical researcher has evoked trance sensations in volunteers by placing special magnets over their heads. However, as the examples on these pages indicate, achieving trances does not require elaborate equipment or special substances. Most are produced through simple but well-practiced physical and mental methods, ranging from wild dancing to quiet, intense meditation.

Whatever its origin, entrancement always entails a suspension of part of the brain's normal functioning, a splitting of consciousness. Everyday awareness of time, change, and death is interrupted, often yielding place to a sublime sense of immortality

When Faith Transcends All

Ecstatic trances are for many people a vital part of religious experience, a way to seek union with the Divine. Devotees of many faiths pursue heightened mystical states through regimens of spiritual devotion and physical purification. The word *mystical* itself comes from a Greek word meaning "to initiate into mystery," into a secret cult.

Many rituals, fasts, and celebrations are meant to help believers attain entrancement. The snake-handling ceremony above, for instance, is performed only after two hours of insistent chanting and cymbal clashing, an entrancing rhythmic din that, some say, lulls the snakes as well as the worshipers into altered states.

Extraordinary occurrences are said to accompany such trances. In most religions, believers have reportedly levitated, gained healing powers, or spontaneously developed physical marks of their faith on their bodies. Spiritual mentors often warn novices not to be seduced by such marvels; they are mere distractions from the true goal of oneness with the Divine.

Saint Catherine of Siena is transfixed by religious ecstasy in this eighteenth-century portrait by Tiepolo. It was said that during a trance she felt the pain of Christ's crucifixion as bleeding wounds— called the stigmata—appeared on her own palms and head.

A Haitian voodoo worshiper dances in a trance, as evidenced by her staring eyes. In voodoo belief, everyday reality masks a spirit world; through ritual drumming, chanting, and dancing, worshipers hope to reach that world and become possessed by gods and spirits.

Surpassing the Body's Limitations

The mind power tapped in trances can lead to remarkable physical accomplishments, feats that seem to rewrite the body's ordinary rules. Many religious regimens use mastery of physical challenges as a step toward the Divine. Some say entrancement is the reason Hindus and others are able to walk barefoot across red-hot coals.

Even with no religious context, the mind power released in a trance can build remarkable physical skills. One American entertainer, strongman Joseph L. Greenstein, "The Mighty Atom," used a kind of trance power to bend iron bars and drive nails with his bare hands. Before performing, he would command the iron: "I am man, you are metal. My will is superior to you. You will bend, you will break."

Western medicine has also discovered the mind-body connection. Amid mounting evidence that states of mind can affect the body's functioning, several cancer clinics teach relaxation and visualization—trance-inducing techniques to help patients strengthen their bodies' defenses against disease.

Tibetan monks wrapped in wet, ice-cold sheets practice Tumo yoga in 40-degree temperatures. During motionless meditation, captured on film in 1985 by Harvard's Herbert Benson, each man purposefully raised his body temperature enough to dry his sheet in forty minutes. They perform the same ritual outdoors in the snow and on cold nights. While Westerners are dazzled by this practice, the monks value it simply as a means of fiery internal purification, leading to a higher state of consciousness.

Culminating an annual Hindu festival in Ceylon, barefoot devotees walk across an eighteen-foot bed of burning embers. Drumming that accompanies the ceremony is said to help the participants enter a state of religious trance.

A Hindu sadhu, or holy man, practices a rare form of meditation, with his head buried in sand, during a 1989 festival at the holy city of Allahabad, India. Deliberately slowing his breathing and heartbeat enabled him to hold this pose for hours. Sadhus perfect such feats as a spiritual discipline

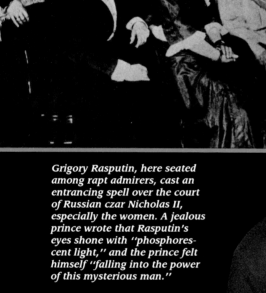

Grigory Rasputin, here seated among rapt admirers, cast an entrancing spell over the court of Russian czar Nicholas II, especially the women. A jealous prince wrote that Rasputin's eyes shone with "phosphorescent light," and the prince felt himself "falling into the power of this mysterious man."

Newspaper heiress Patricia Hearst strikes a militant pose before the emblem of the Symbionese Liberation Army, a radical group that kidnapped her in 1974. When she joined her captors in armed robbery and kidnapping, her parents insisted she had been brainwashed—in effect, entranced.

Bhagwan Shree Rajneesh (below) ministers to ecstatic followers at his ashram in Poona, India, shortly before his death in 1990. Earlier, at his Oregon commune, the guru held 6,000 disciples in abject thrall and enjoyed the use of ninety-three Rolls-Royces provided for him.

The Rev. and Mrs. Sun Myung Moon (inset, top left) officiate at the biggest mass wedding in history (above) at Madison Square Garden in 1982. These 4,150 members of Moon's Unification Church proved their unswerving loyalty by allowing him to select their spouses.

Minds in Thrall

The human urge to dominate others is ancient and powerful; manipulating another's mind is for some irresistible. Yet seemingly just as strong is the impulse to fall under another's spell, to surrender volition and obey without question. Some authorities view such subjection as a trance.

The partnership may be constructive, as when a patient submits willingly to a hypnotic trance. At the other extreme are vulnerable captives victimized by brainwashing. In between lies a shadowy area where ostensibly free people are manipulated by a forcefully charismatic individual who exerts a kind of religious power without providing the rewards of traditional faiths.

Research suggests that people who join control-oriented cults are emotionally unstable or in the midst of a crisis that inclines them to surrender command of their lives. Subjected to repetitive drills, long hours of wearisome work, sleep deprivation, and often a restricted diet, a person can easily slide into a state of numb submission, a nightmarish chronic trance.

CHAPTER 4

The Outer Limits

Ridden with dysentery and shaking with fever, John Bennett awoke one summer morning in 1923 resigned to spending the day in bed. Then suddenly he became charged with an immense, inexplicable power: "I felt my body rising, I dressed and went to work as usual, but this time with a queer sense of being held together by a superior Will that was not my own."

Bennett's newfound strength carried him through a morning of work, but by lunchtime he felt too ill to eat, and an afternoon exercise class seemed beyond his endurance. Yet Bennett felt compelled to participate. By profession a scientist and mathematician, he had recently become a disciple of Georgei Gurdjieff's at the Greco-Armenian mystic's Institute for the Harmonious Development of Man in Fontainebleau, just outside Paris, and the exercises were an important part of the program. Gurdjieff's prescribed movements were enormously complex and required great concentration and coordination, but Bennett forced himself to follow the program even as other students dropped out one by one. Near exhaustion himself, Bennett suddenly felt another great surge of power, an even more intense charge than the one he had experienced that morning. "My body seemed to have turned into light," he said. "I could not feel its presence in the usual ways. There was no effort, no pain, no weariness, not even any sense of weight."

To test the extent of this mysterious vitality, Bennett went from exercise class to his garden and began digging in the fierce heat of the afternoon. He started at a pace that would ordinarily exhaust him in just a few minutes, but he felt no fatigue, no sense of effort. Furthermore, his mental state was different. "I experienced a clarity of thought that I had only known involuntarily and at rare moments, but which was now at my command. . . . The phrase 'in my mind's eye' took on a new meaning as I 'saw' the eternal pattern of each thing I looked at; the trees, the plants, the water flowing in the canal and even the spade, and lastly my own body."

Later, while walking in a nearby forest, Bennett discovered another aspect of the curious power that had overtaken him. He recalled a lecturer who had pointed out how little control humans have over their emotions, citing as proof the fact that one cannot be astonished at will. But when

Bennett said to himself "I will be astonished," he was instantly overwhelmed with amazement about everything he looked at or thought of. "Each tree was so uniquely itself that I felt I could walk in the forest forever and never cease from wonderment. Then the thought of 'fear' came to me. At once I was shaking with terror. Unknown horrors were menacing me on every side. I thought of 'joy' and I felt that my heart would burst from rapture. The word 'love' came to me, and I was pervaded with such fine shades of tenderness and compassion that I saw that I had not the remotest idea of the depth and range of love. Love was everywhere and in everything. It was infinitely adaptable to every shade of need. After a time, it became too much for me; it seemed that if I plunged any more deeply into the mystery of love, I would cease to exist. I wanted to be free from this power to feel whatever I chose, and at once it left me."

Bennett's experience of transcending the limits of the everyday mind was precisely the point of Georgei Gurdjieff's rigorous exercises. As a young man Gurdjieff had wandered for years through India, Tibet, and the Middle East searching for ways to tap the full potential of human existence. He came to believe that although most people take the limits of their lives for granted, they can in fact be awakened to an understanding of great unused powers within themselves.

The system that he eventually taught in Russia, in France, and in the United States blended elements of Sufism, Buddhism, and Christianity; at its center were the complex exercises requiring such intense concentration that participants might sometimes unknowingly venture beyond their perceived boundaries and discover greater awareness and control. As they moved to ever-higher levels within their own minds, Gurdjieff taught, they would be increasingly open to visions of a mental and physical life untethered by the trivialities of day-to-day existence.

Gurdjieff's technique for expanding the apparent confines of consciousness is one of many strategies devised by humans over the centuries to explore the frontiers of the mind and tap its unused potential. To the mystics of India and Tibet, many levels of consciousness exist above humankind's normal, self-centered state. The levels ascend, with growing transcendence and broadening consciousness, to a state of enlightenment in which the ego, or self, has been left far behind. At the highest level, adherents believe, is nirvana, to which all life aspires. Sometimes described as a union with the ultimate principle of the universe, nirvana is not just personal salvation, but participation in a reality that goes beyond birth and death.

Virtually every culture known to history has found ways to diffuse the normal focus of the mind and extend its perceptions to the outer reaches—to give precedence, as it were, to the mind's peripheral vision. So widespread has humankind's pursuit of altered states of consciousness been that some scholars speculate it may be an innate impulsion akin to hunger or the sexual drive. The path of many searchers has been the cere-

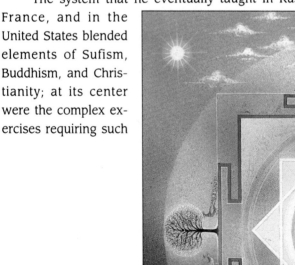

monial pursuit of mystical and religious revelation. For most Buddhists this constitutes a lifetime of discipline and meditation. The ancient Hindus, however, are said to have used an occasional chemical shortcut: Their religious rites sometimes included a beverage called soma, which produced an altered state replete with vivid hallucinations and sensations of power and knowledge.

Westerners historically have been less inclined toward mystical explorations of consciousness. Yet an articulate few have pursued similar transcendent experiences, both self-induced and aided by drugs. Saints and poets alike have spoken of visions that opened their minds briefly to the peaceful, joyous contemplation of the boundless universe and their essential unity with it. William Blake, an English artist and poet born in 1757, first experienced such visions as a child in London and went on to produce a body of work that extolled the expansion of the mind beyond its ordinary role of monitoring and responding to the senses. "If the doors of perception were cleansed," Blake wrote, "every thing would appear to man as it is—infinite."

Psychologist and philosopher William James took a more academic approach to the subject in his work at Harvard University in the late nineteenth century. He believed that psychologists should aim to describe and explain the whole spectrum of consciousness. Normal waking awareness, he taught, was but one state, separated from entirely different states only "by the filmiest of screens." James parted the screens for himself in experiments with nitrous oxide, an anesthetic known as laughing gas, and in *The Varieties of Religious Experience,* published in 1902, he pointed out the similarities of raptures induced by drugs and those arrived at by mystical means.

James presaged later generations for whom access to higher regions of the mind had implications beyond the mystical and religious insights of the visionaries. Psychologists hoped to find new ways of liberating patients from debilitating mental afflictions, and self-help advocates touted the potential of moving beyond ordinary consciousness to boost learning power, improve motivation, and

increase achievement in fields as diverse as sports and business.

In the drug-laced euphoria of the 1960s, Western converts expected expanded forms of consciousness to create a new society in which material obsessions would be abandoned in favor of spiritual values. And when that dream dissolved in the political and social reaction to the era, the

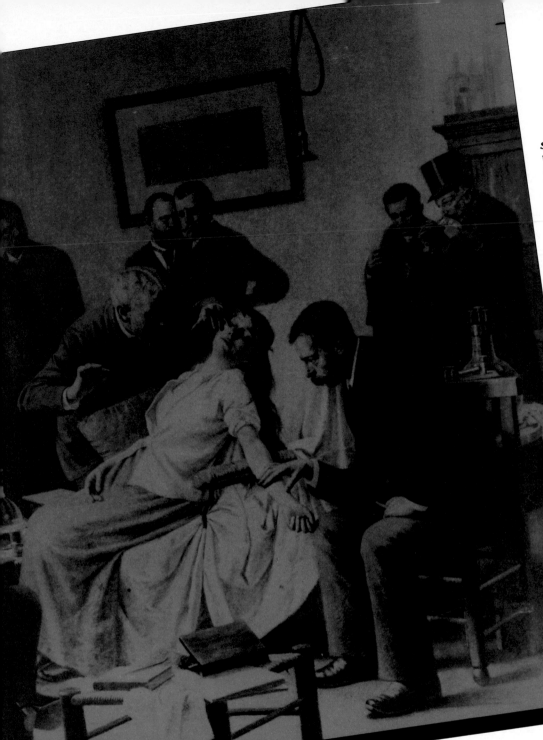

Surrounded by concerned physicians, a woman swoons into the sleeplike trance of hypnosis in this 1893 painting. A state in which the subconscious seems to dominate the conscious mind, hypnosis was used by some nineteenth-century doctors to anesthetize and to treat nervous disorders.

As William James pointed out, the various altered states share certain qualities; the differences are mainly of intensity. Whether they get there by way of whirling dances or meditation, many people in altered states of mind experience a sense of timelessness and physical lightness. Many report being suffused in a golden glow that stretches from horizon to horizon. Paradoxically, the altered state also often produces a narrowed focus of attention, a zeroing in on specifics.

In the continuum of consciousness, a trance, whether spontaneous or hypnotic, is an extension of daydreaming; meditation, though voluntary and purposeful, is hard to distinguish from a trance. A moviegoer who becomes oblivious to everything but the screen, for instance, is in a light trance; his or her awareness is more intense but is more restricted than in ordinary consciousness. Marijuana users have described their increased internal focus and detachment from the outside world with the analogy of an old-fashioned telephone switchboard in which all but one or two of the incoming trunk lines have been disconnnected.

When the power of such a state increases and the scope of consciousness narrows, unusual phenomena begin to appear, such as the blocking of pain signals. A deep trance—one induced by hypnosis, for example—can in some cases substitute for chemical anesthesia during major

yearning for transcendental enlightenment led many people to seek it through other means. Some focused on the demanding, ascetic way of Eastern mystics; others hoped to expand the mind's borders through science and technology. In recent decades a brand-new frontier of inquiry has been opened by the ever-growing ability of computers to mimic functions that had long been thought unique to the human mind. Still others embraced more mundane efforts at mind expansion, including sleep, daydreaming, trance, and hypnosis.

surgery. Apparently the patient's consciousness is so tightly focused that the pain generated by the surgeon's knife is momentarily outside the boundary of consciousness.

Most altered states also produce a major change in the sense of ego—a person's routine awareness of existing as a discrete entity. With the onset of a reverie, for instance, the monitoring self disappears; when the daydreamer snaps back to the here and now, the individual wonders where he or she has been for the past few minutes. Precisely this forgetfulness of self is at the core of some religions and systems of mind development.

Zen Buddhists sometimes use archery as a spiritual exercise. According to Zen master D. T. Suzuki, the meditating archer "ceases to be conscious of himself as the one who is engaged in hitting the bull's eye which confronts him." Ideally, the archer eliminates the distinctions between himself, the bow, the arrow, and the target, so that hitting the target is no more difficult than reaching out and touching it. In Zen, the goal is not physical success, but the state of mind required to achieve it. Nevertheless, the capacity to forget oneself is an important factor in perfecting any skill. A true master—artisan, artist, performer—forsakes the ego-centered focus of normal waking consciousness and becomes "lost in the work," much as John Bennett did during his exercises at Gurdjieff's institute.

Although various ancient cultures in the search for revelation have used what in today's jargon are called controlled substances—such as the soma of the Hindus—it is a fairly recent preoccupation in the West to view medications that affect the mind as tools for scientifically exploring higher consciousness. Many reputable researchers have worked to prove that mental changes produced by these psychoactive drugs can provide insight into the brain's perceptual equipment and illuminate normally shadowy parts of the psyche. They have a complicated task.

In the period following World War II, well before the serious physical and emotional side effects of drug use were so widely known, researchers began to tinker with a class of drugs called hallucinogenics. They discovered that these substances, including drugs such as psilocybin and lysergic acid diethylamide—which entered everyday language during the 1960s as LSD—were capable of producing powerful hallucinations in tiny doses. The first documented LSD "trip," as the mind-expanding excursions later became known, was made in 1943 by a Swiss chemist named Albert Hofmann, who took a mere quarter of a milligram of the drug and stumbled into a realm of startling revelation. "To see the flowers in my own garden is to see all the mystical wonder of creation," Hofmann marveled after his pioneering experiment.

Later researchers followed up on Hofmann's beatific experience, often with much broader goals in view. Much of the early funding for experiments in the United States, in fact, came from government agencies. The Central Intelligence Agency, interested in the hallucinogenics' potential as weapons that could break down the defenses of enemy agents and unlock the lips of trained spies, in the early 1950s subsidized studies in which witting and unwitting subjects—sometimes CIA officials themselves—were given food or drink laced with drugs such as LSD. Their research revealed that in addition to causing kaleidoscopic visions, the drugs at times seemed to produce effects similar to psychosis. Yet the testing continued in one form or another until the mid-1960s. By then, however, agency officials had to admit that while LSD penetrated the innermost reaches of the mind, it unleashed such a gamut of human reactions and emotions that even the most skilled manipulator could not claim control over the minds of those who ingested it.

Aldous Huxley, a British novelist and philosopher, tested the effects of cactus-derived mescaline on his own psyche and recorded his observations in the 1954 essay *The Doors of Perception,* which took its title from William Blake. Huxley recounted floods of pleasurable sensations, such as "a slow dance of golden lights," and described the flashes of "transcendental otherness" he experienced while riding in a car through a Los Angeles suburb under the drug's in-

Bizarre apparitions assail a young man under the mind-altering influence of ether. Such alarming hallucinations were among the unpleasant side effects that led physicians to abandon ether as a general anesthetic soon after its discovery in the mid-1800s, around the time this etching was made.

fluence. A stucco wall with a slanting shadow across it, for example, was "blank but unforgettably beautiful, empty but charged with all the meaning and the mystery of existence. The revelation dawned and was gone again within a fraction of a second."

The incredible flow of sensory information let loose by the mescaline led Huxley to the hypothesis that the main function of the brain and nervous system is that of a reducing valve to restrict the input of reality to a manageable level. He surmised that so much data is available through the five senses that if all of it were processed the mind would be overwhelmed, incapable of dealing with the problems of everyday life.

The mescaline, Huxley believed, disabled the brain's filtering function, allowing the mind to become flooded with mental events that are usually excluded because they have no survival value. These intrusions, he wrote, are "biologically useless, but aesthetically and sometimes spiritually valuable." He believed them to be representations of what he called Mind at Large, an awareness of everything happening everywhere in the universe. Furthermore, he suggested, they can be stimulated by a catalyst other than drugs, such as illness, fatigue, fasting, or complete sensory withdrawal in a dark, silent place.

Whatever the means of achieving them, Huxley believed that humanity needed these "artificial paradises." He opined that "most men and women lead lives at the worst so painful, at the best so monotonous, poor and limited that the urge to escape, the longing to transcend themselves if only for a few moments, is and has always been one of the principal appetites of the soul. Art and religion, carnivals and saturnalia, dancing and listening to oratory—all these have served, in H. G. Wells's phrase, as Doors in the Wall. And for private, for everyday use there have always been chemical intoxicants. All the vegetable sedatives and narcotics, all the euphorics that grow on trees, the hallucinogens that ripen in berries or can be squeezed from roots—all, without exception, have been known and systematically used by human beings from time immemorial."

Huxley seems to have been close to the mark in his idea of the brain as a filter. Modern research has shown that two substances in the brain—serotonin and norepinephrine—act as switches that control the signals the cortex sends the brain. When the system's norepinephrine is increased or the serotonin reduced, the switches are changed so that the cortex is titillated and the brain is destabilized. Apparently LSD does in fact have this effect. The reduction filter is knocked out, and the brain is free to produce its own internal landscape of images—hallucinations.

Huxley was convinced of the good effects of his mescaline experience, although he did not equate it, or any other drug experience, with the true enlightenment that he, by then a practicing Buddhist, considered to be "the end and ultimate purpose of human life." But he believed drugs could assist toward that end, pharmacologically providing a spiritual state that Catholic theologians call "a gratuitous grace"—something that, though not necessary to salvation, may be helpful. "To be shaken out of the ruts of ordinary perception," wrote Huxley, "to be shown for a few timeless hours the outer and the inner world, not as they appear to an animal obsessed with survival or to a human being obsessed with words and notions, but as they are apprehended, directly and unconditionally, by Mind at Large—this is an experience of inestimable value to everyone."

Still, Huxley chose to tread lightly in extolling the potential benefits of mind-expanding drugs. He predicted—rightly, as it turned out—strong resistance to his ideas from the dominant Western culture, with its strongly rational foundations. Yet experimental research continued with the drugs, which came to be called psychedelics (an apt adaptation of Greek words meaning "mind made visible"), and other proselytes for chemical enlightenment were less circumspect than Huxley. One, a psychologist named Timothy Leary, eventually came to embody a revolutionary spirit of mental exploration.

Leary was a well-regarded—if somewhat flamboyant—teacher and researcher in 1958 when he resigned from

his position as director of psychological research at the Kaiser Foundation Hospital in Oakland, California. Personally and professionally, Leary's life was in turmoil. Three years earlier, his disintegrating marriage had ended when his wife committed suicide; at the same time, he was trying to come to grips with the apparent failures of his chosen field. In ten years of keeping score, Leary and his staff had found that no matter what method they used, the patients they treated did about as well as those they did not—one-third got better, one-third got worse, and one-third stayed about the same.

Leaving California with a small research grant and some cash from insurance policies, Leary moved to Europe with his two children and spent a year "reading philosophy and thinking." The result was the manuscript of a book called *The Existential Transaction,* in which Leary suggested new means for changing behavior. He favored a humanist approach, with researchers learning about the mind by working with people in real-life situations, a method similar to that of a naturalist in the field. Rather than simply examining, diagnosing, and treating patients, he wanted psychologists to help them by emphasizing inner potential and change through self-reliance. To do so, practitioners would have to become involved with their subjects, he counseled, and be prepared "to change as much or more than the subjects being studied."

While living in Florence, Leary met David McClelland, the director of the Harvard Center for Personality Research, who was visiting Italy on a sabbatical leave. McClelland had read Leary's earlier work on psychotherapy and was impressed by it; after listening to his new ideas, the director offered him a job on the spot. Leary would teach a graduate seminar on psychotherapy.

Leary was a maverick from the day he arrived on the Harvard campus in Cambridge, Massachusetts. He complemented his professorial tweeds with white sneakers (he was later described by Albert Hofmann as looking more like a tennis champion than a Harvard lecturer) and engaged in endless late-night discussions with students over half-gallon jugs of California wine. He soon gathered around

him a group of young scholars impatient with the established approaches to changing human nature—the best of which seemed far too slow. Leary had strong reservations, though, when one graduate student told him of experiments with the drug mescaline; Leary disapproved of such chemical meddling with the natural psyche.

That conservative attitude changed in the summer of 1960, however. Before he left for a vacation in Mexico, Leary talked with Frank Barron, a longtime California friend who would soon be coming to Harvard as a visiting professor. On a recent visit to Mexico, Barron had obtained some hallucinogenic "magic mushrooms" from a psychiatrist. The mystical insights and perspectives that Barron experienced after eating the fungi led him to believe they might be the instruments for behavioral change that he and Leary had often discussed. Leary remained skeptical, but when he was offered the chance to try some mushrooms in Mexico, he was quick to accept.

The mushrooms were bitter and stringy, with a smell that reminded Leary of a moldy New England basement. He gulped six, washing them down with beer, then sat back around a swimming pool with a group of friends to wait for the effects. Soon he began to feel strange: mildly nauseated, detached from his fellow mushroom eaters. Gradually the rest of the world, even inanimate objects, began quivering with life. Glancing at an abstaining friend who was taking notes, Leary burst into uproarious laughter as he realized that the watcher had no idea what he was observing. "I laughed again at my own everyday pomposity," Leary later wrote, "the narrow arrogance of scholars, the impudence of the rational, the smug naivete of words in contrast to the raw rich ever-changing panoramas that flooded my brain. . . . I gave way to delight, as mystics have for centuries when they peeked through the curtains and discovered that this world—so manifestly real—was actually a tiny stage set constructed by the mind. There was a sea of possibilities out there (in there?), other realities, an infinite array of programs for other futures."

The tropical liana plant (right), or ayahuasca, is one of the two plants Amazonian shamans combine in their potent hallucinogenic drink, also known as ayahuasca. In the painting below, the mixing of the ayahuasca and chacruna plants is depicted by the impending union of two snakes. To the left of the snakes, a shaman and his disciples sit around a pot of ayahuasca brew, enveloped in the energy of the vines. At right, smoking his snake-shaped pipe, stands the gardener who tends the ayahuasca plant. The skulls warn those who would partake of the potent brew without the proper knowledge and reverence.

Visions of a Hallucinogenic Jungle

Beyond ordinary reality and the boundaries of the everyday mind, say the Amazonian shamans, lies a world of spirit guides, sorcerers, magical illnesses, and magical cures. They reach this world with the help of a vision-inducing drug extracted from local plants. Mixed into a drink called ayahuasca and sipped in prescribed doses, the hallucinogen appears to open gates to other realms. Some say ayahuasca—also called the vine of death—is so powerful that its visions can kill a careless user with fear.

During fifteen years as a *vegetalista*—or "plant healer"—Peruvian painter Pablo Amaringo regularly drank aya-huasca. From the vivid mental images it produced, he claims to have learned how to cure illnesses and how to mix colors for his paintings. In 1975, threatened by shamans who envied his powers, Amaringo forsook his vegetalista practice and the potent ayahuasca. But he still recalled his visions clearly enough to paint them.

In 1985, visiting scholar Luis Eduardo Luna urged Amaringo to describe more of his visions on canvas and in words. The works shown here and on the following pages are taken from a book by the two called *Ayahuasca Visions: The Religious Iconography of Pablo Amaringo, a Peruvian Shaman.*

*Like the colored arcs of a brilliant rain-
bow, the hierarchy of powers in the invisible world is revealed in Amaringo's
painting. Starting with the green arc,
containing animals and plants known to
novice shamans, each band represents
more transcendent knowledge. In the
pinkish arc are hypnotic animals and
fortunetellers; the blue arc holds angels
with extrasensory powers; and in the
violet arc are kings, queens, fairies, and
muses. Tiny by comparison, the vegetalistas at lower left drink ayahuasca to
learn about the array of powers. The
circles around their hut symbolize icaros,
magical songs that summon the visions.*

Queen Pulsarium Coya grants four vegetalistas the power to diagnose patients by
"pulsing"—feeling their pulses. She has
also given them animal guardians, seen
clinging to their sleeves, who will help
the shamans identify various maladies.
The bands snaking across the painting
represent the healers' brain waves moving in synchrony with their patients'
pulsations; above the bands, the forest
teems with spirits associated with pulsing. At top right, above the bearded men,
hovers a UFO from a realm vegetalistas
are said to visit when using ayahuasca.

Good and evil face off in the dramatic painting below as a sorcerer and his bat-shaped evil spirit (upper left) prepare to attack a gathering of vegetalistas. In addition to the bat spirit, who is sending sonic waves to make his victims sleepy, the sorcerer's nefarious allies include evil fireflies, deadly house lizards, and red-necked sorcerer birds. The shaman, who is shown wearing a protective design on his back and spewing dazzling waves of color to blind his enemy, is also aided by an army of spirits, including a snake toad and the parrot snake (lower left), whose human arms hurl poisoned daggers.

Calling on their helping spirits, a master vegetalista and his two apprentices (above) use various healing methods. The master, kneeling over his patient, calls on his powerful white phlegm to extract magical darts from a woman's stomach. At center, an apprentice fans a woman with an achote plant to cure her of a fright caused by an evil spirit. A second apprentice sings over a love-struck man (seated) who has fallen ill because he used a love charm improperly. Aiding the apprentice are the spirits of the red goat, whose breath has curative powers, and a snake (top right) that will draw out the man's insanity.

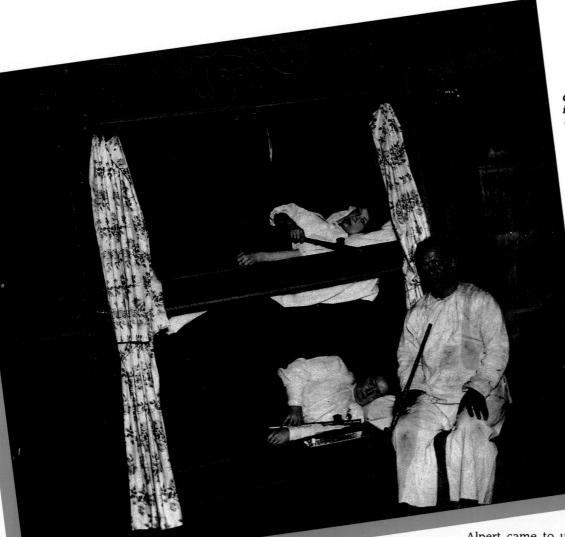

Clutching pipes, three addicts drift into a drug-induced stupor in a turn-of-the-century opium den in New York's Chinatown. Smoked, eaten, or sipped as tea throughout history, opium is an addictive narcotic derived from the same poppy that yields morphine and heroin.

the drugs, he and his team could use them to explore the true essence of psychology, aesthetics, philosophy, religion—even life itself.

By the spring of 1961, Leary and fellow Harvard researcher Richard Alpert had administered psychedelic drugs to more than 200 subjects. They discovered a broad range of responses, not only in different subjects, but even during different occasions for the same subject. Leary and Alpert came to understand that these vagaries were determined by the dosage of the drug as well as by two variables they called "set" and "setting." Set refers to a person's expectations of the drug's effects, setting to the physical and social environment in which the drug is taken. By insisting on the importance of these variables, Leary and Alpert were able to isolate more accurately the real—as opposed to the subjective—effects of the drugs.

Despite the variety of experiences, a vast majority of the subjects reported positive reactions: 85 percent of them said the experience was the most educational of their lives. There was no way of demonstrating, however, that any of the subjects' lives were actually permanently improved, and Leary and Alpert looked for a situation that would provide an objective index. They found it in a nearby state prison, where they were invited to see if they could help inmates change the patterns of their lives. The first prison volunteers were an intimidating lot—two murderers, two armed robbers, an embezzler, and a

Leary's journey beyond the normal limits of his mind lasted about four hours, and he returned profoundly changed. He felt he had done more in this short trip to investigate the vast unexplored realms of the brain than he had in his fifteen previous years as a psychologist. Like Georgei Gurdjieff before him, he became convinced that the brain is underutilized and capable of being reprogrammed for greatly expanded intelligence and consciousness. Instead of Gurdjieff's exercises, though, Leary regarded psychedelic drugs as the key to achieving and analyzing these higher levels of awareness. As one researcher put it, the drugs would provide a "pharmacological bridge to transcendence."

Returning to Harvard, Leary established a research program to explore the matter further. He legally obtained a quantity of psilocybin, the active ingredient of the mushrooms, and worked out a plan of interactive participation in which his investigators took the drugs along with their subjects. Leary believed that once they learned to accurately chart the mind wanderings prompted by various doses of

Cocaine was the active ingredient of a "digestive tonic" promoted as a beauty secret in this late-1800s French poster. While it renders a euphoric state of mind, cocaine can also confer a powerful addiction, paranoid psychosis, and fatal convulsions.

heroin dealer—and Leary's work with them started off on the wrong foot. The setting of the cold, sunless penitentiary was depressing, and when Leary admitted his fear of the criminals, one inmate responded by describing his own counterproductive feeling, a fear of the "mad scientist." Suddenly laughter filled the room, and the session turned into an enlightening one for all the participants; the convicts experienced the same mind-opening phenomena that the graduate students had.

In the program's second year, the convicts appeared to benefit from their insights: They perceived new possibilities for life outside of prison and were given considerable emotional support in the parole period by the Harvard project coordinators. Many succeeded on their new paths; within a year of release, only about 10 percent of those paroled wound up in prison again, whereas 70 percent of their untreated peers returned to jail.

While the prison project continued in 1962, Leary took part in another, radically different study. Collaborating with Walter Pahnke, a young medical doctor studying religion, he set up an experiment to test the effect of psilocybin on the intensity of the mystical and religious experience. The session took place on Good Friday in the chapel of Boston University, with twenty carefully briefed theology students as subjects. Half of the students were given the drug, and the other half took a dummy pill; none were told which they had taken. All listened to a long religious service with organ and vocal music, readings, prayers, and personal meditation. Pahnke collected data from the participants for six months and discovered distinct differences between the two test groups. He checked the subjects' description of their experience on that Good Friday against a list of sensations that had been recounted by mystics in other circum-

stances, such as ineffability—the failure of words to express the experience—and a sense of transcendence of time and space. On every count, those who took psilocybin showed far greater intensity of religious experience than those in the control group; fully half of the drug takers reported lasting positive changes in their attitudes and behavior as a result of the Good Friday session.

These encouraging results convinced Leary and Albert that psychedelic drugs could play a key role in transforming society. They wrote a manual for their mystical undertakings entitled *The Psychedelic Journey*, choosing as their model the *Bardo Thodol,* or Tibetan *Book of the Dead*. This great Buddhist text, aimed at the living, spells out all the levels of consciousness leading up to the "clear light of illumination," a transcendent state of liberation from the ego. Leary showed the parallels between these levels and the altered states induced by psychedelic drugs, and he hopefully predicted that one way his scientific drug program could work for the good of society was by helping people explore the sacred realms of the mind.

Leary soon learned, however, that society did not want to be transformed. His drug-tinted panacea was poison to the establishment. Influential members of the Harvard faculty were alienated by the project's flamboyantly rebellious image and by Leary's own high profile as a promoter of the new consciousness. There was also trouble with the administration at the university; deans were fielding many complaints from parents whose children phoned home to announce that they had discovered the secret of the universe.

It made little difference that these undergraduates were not part of Leary's project, which involved only grad-

A sequence of drawings of a man's face, done after the artist swallowed the hallucinogen known as LSD, progresses from realistic to fractured to fluidly abstract. Part of a 1951 German experiment, the series captures the extreme psychic changes the drug can induce.

uate students. Drug consciousness was spreading among American youth, and psychedelic drugs were easy to find; some enterprising chemistry students began to set up home laboratories to meet the demand. And as Leary himself admitted, parents did not necessarily send their sons and daughters to Harvard to become buddhas.

Matters came to a head in the spring of 1963, when Leary and Alpert were dismissed from the Harvard faculty, a step rarely taken in the university's 300-year history. The backlash in Cambridge spread to other parts of the nation, wherever researchers had been engaged in similar experiments. By 1966, stringent new laws and regulations brought psychedelic research to a virtual halt; scientists were asked to return their supplies of the drugs to the manufacturers. Leary, who after leaving Harvard became a sort of freelance preacher of altered states, was a marked man, hounded by police as well as by politicians.

Arrested for possession of less than an ounce of marijuana, Timothy Leary eventually served a prison sentence, which was made substantially longer by a dashing escape that took him to Europe and on to North Africa before he was captured and returned to jail. Throughout the ordeal, however, he retained his faith in the intelligent use of mind-altering drugs as a means for personal and societal improvement.

Opponents of the drug restrictions saw them as desperate attempts by an ego-centered establishment to ensure its survival. Proponents of the new

LSD guru Timothy Leary touted hallucinogenic drugs as a "road to happiness," one with "almost limitless possibilities for the expansion of the human mind." Ironically, Leary's brash experiments helped bring about tighter legal restrictions on the use of mind-altering drugs.

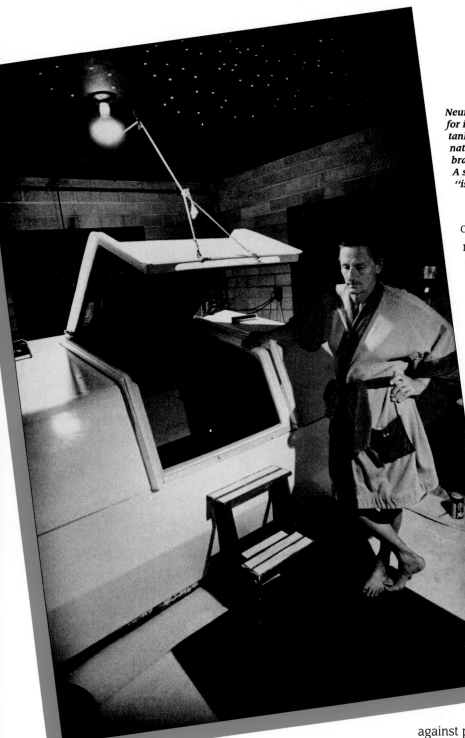

oped during the 1960s, LSD maintained the sacramental status that Leary had ascribed to it. Furthermore, like the prisoners and theology students Leary treated with the drug, many felt that the psychedelic experience profoundly changed their lives for the better.

Despite the dire warnings of the anti-LSD forces, very little solid evidence has emerged to prove that psychedelic drugs typically cause lasting damage, either physical or psychic. Although flashbacks (recurrences of LSD's effects), chronic anxiety states, and schizophrenia-like psychoses sometimes occur after frequent exposure to the drug, the questions of brain cell or chromosome damage have not yet been satisfactorily answered on a scientific basis. In fact, according to scientists who stoutly defend their drug-related research, mind-altering substances such as LSD, to say nothing of the nonhallucinogenic marijuana, are positively benign compared with those much more dangerous drugs of choice, alcohol and tobacco.

Still, anyone in an altered state of consciousness is also in a vulnerable state, whatever means were used to reach that condition. The normal defenses against physical and psychic dangers are relaxed, and dangerous—sometimes tragic—situations arise. Converts at religious revival meetings, in an ecstatic longing to be reborn, have thrown themselves into rivers and drowned; innumerable cases of "possession" tell of victims who inflicted wounds on themselves or others while in the grip of an alternate personality; sleepwalkers have sauntered along perilously high balconies. Leary tells of an episode in the early days of his experimental work with LSD in which a subject took the drug even though both the set and the setting were negative. The subject spent the next several hours bounding around like a gorilla, climbing drainpipes and swinging in

laws believed that psychedelics were dangerous drugs that should be administered only by physicians in a medical setting. The prohibitionists had a point: As Leary and Alpert had learned in their investigation of set and setting, psychedelics could unleash powerful negative reactions in people who were ill prepared for the experience or who took the drugs in hostile environments.

Nevertheless, the drug ban had little effect on the rising tide of personal experimentation with psychedelics. For many youths in the substantial counterculture that devel-

trees, covering himself with cuts and bruises. It was one of the first "bad trips" that Leary witnessed, and it convinced him that strict controls over the set and setting of experiments, as well as over the purity of the drugs, must always be maintained.

But there was yet another problem with using psychedelics as a key to revelation. Even those who defend the use of drugs as a tool for positive mind expansion have had to admit that the glorious effects of drug-induced consciousness altering are all too often temporary. Again and again the exhilarating revelations of a drug experience have faded with the light of dawn. As philosopher and author Arthur Koestler put it in 1960, after trying psilocybin with Leary in Cambridge, "I solved the secret of the universe last night, but this morning I forgot what it was."

So, pressured by antidrug laws and disillusioned by the ephemeral effects of their magic pills, devotees began to look for other methods of pursuing their spiritual goals. Many turned back to the meditative practices of Eastern religions. Like Aldous Huxley before them, they found that the highs reached by meditation were purer and longer lasting than those obtained through drugs. Meditation is also devoid of the physical side effects of drugs, such as dilated eyes, cold hands, nausea, and wakefulness, which have nothing to do with the desired mental state.

Furthermore, while drugs seemed to reveal new dimensions of the mind, they also reinforced the illusion that those dimensions were accessible only by external, material means. Mystics—and some drug researchers—believe that those dimensions are actually available to anyone, anytime, even though most people do not know how to reach them without drugs. The goal of meditation is to overcome illusion and to know that higher levels of consciousness come from the mind itself.

Richard Alpert discovered the power of meditative highs when he traveled to India in 1967 to find out how Eastern holy men reacted to psychedelics. In the foothills of the Himalayas he displayed his treasured stock of LSD to yoga master Neem Karoli Baba—who promptly consumed it

all. The astonished Alpert saw no effect whatsoever on the holy man from the drug, enough for dozens of ordinary psychedelic excursions. When someone explained that the holy man operated at a level of consciousness that did not depend on physical or biological stimulation, Alpert realized he had come upon a spiritual source well beyond his previous experience.

Alpert stayed in India for a year, living in a small hut, bathing each morning in the icy water of a mountain stream, and filling his days with yoga exercises assigned by the guru. Returning to the United States as Baba Ram Dass, he became a popular lecturer and author, communicating the wisdom of the East to Western audiences.

Those audiences included more than the veterans of the psychedelic revolution. Many people who had never used drugs were also eager to find a safe way to explore the outer reaches of their minds. Not everyone, however, was prepared to take Alpert's ascetic route to transformation; many were put off by the persistence and effort required to expand their consciousness through meditation. There remained a demand for mind-altering methods with the power and immediacy of drugs but without their dangers, and by the end of the 1960s, more typically American paths to higher consciousness were beginning to emerge.

John Lilly was a leading figure in this movement to map inner space. Trained as a medical doctor, he performed research in fields as diverse as biophysics, neurophysiology, electronics, and neuroanatomy. Lilly also garnered substantial fame for his work on relations between humans and dolphins, fictionalized on film in 1973's *The Day of the Dolphin*. His interest in dolphins grew from an experiment he conducted in 1954, while working at the National Institute for Mental Health near Washington, D.C. To test a then-current theory that people remain awake only if they are continuously bombarded by sensory stimuli, Lilly decided to put himself in an environment with the minimum possible sensory input. He found a water tank in a small, soundproof room that he filled with water at 93 degrees Fahrenheit—the temperature at which

Resplendently garbed, Telsen-Sao leader Jeshahr the Guide (left) exudes a cosmic authority that transcends his earlier careers as dishwasher and bank employee. His sleeve insignia, the winged lion of San Marco, represents peaceful intent—a key to safe out-of-body travel.

A School for Astral Travelers

I found myself in an indefinable sphere of feelings and music. Every image became small like the head of a pin and then split into an endless number of visions, sometimes like paradise, sometimes monstrous. The shadows of a thousand hands tried to catch me, but I was flying very fast." Thus did a young man called Nirvan describe the curious mental journey he undertook in 1988 at Telsen-Sao, a quasi-military school in Italy devoted to the training of out-of-body travelers.

Throughout the ages, a few sensitive people have said their consciousness could at times slip away in an insubstantial "astral body," a weightless form capable of flying off at great speeds and then returning to the physical body. But those who run Telsen-Sao (an Italian acronym for "extrasensory learning") claim to have transformed that personal phenomenon into an ability attainable through proper instruction and rigid discipline—an assertion apparently accepted by students, despite uniforms and equipment that lend the institution an air of a low-budget 1950s sci-fi thriller.

Telsen-Sao cadets study such topics as cosmic navigation, geography, and a supposedly universal language called Jeshaele. That preparation is potentially lifesaving, says the school's founder, Renato Minozzi, now known as Jeshahr the Guide. Claiming to have first left his own body during a 1971 coma, Jeshahr believes that untrained astral travelers risk becoming forever lost in "other spheres"—such as the realms of the dead and the immortal. At last report, no cadets had failed to return from a mission.

Under a glowing ankhlike emblem that combines a cross, a crescent, and a star of David, students in the Celestial Abyss course plot their astral flight paths. Telsen-Sao navigation methods involve sound, color, radio waves, and a complex pyramidal coordinate system.